He shoved the door open to survey the damage and check for any sign of life.

Nothing.

He blew out a long breath, trying to drag enough oxygen into his lungs to breathe. It took Caleb another second to realize Avery had never let go of his shirt.

"We're okay," Caleb said.

"I can't believe…" Her voice shook as hard as her body.

Reality came roaring back. This was his life, not hers. She'd held it together, helped him. When everything fell apart around her, she held it together. In that moment, their history didn't matter.

Knowing it was stupid he leaned down and placed a quick kiss on her lips. Once his lips met her soft mouth, the temptation to linger and relearn the taste of her grabbed him, but he pushed it out of his head. This was about providing comfort, ~~not~~ ~~a~~ moment to celeb~~rate~~

D1462630

HELENKAY DIMON

GUNNING FOR TROUBLE

TORONTO NEW YORK LONDON
AMSTERDAM PARIS SYDNEY HAMBURG
STOCKHOLM ATHENS TOKYO MILAN MADRID
PRAGUE WARSAW BUDAPEST AUCKLAND

To my mom, Joan Dimon, who loves reading mysteries, thrillers and romantic suspense as much as I do.

Recycling programs
for this product may
not exist in your area.

ISBN-13: 978-0-373-69527-0

GUNNING FOR TROUBLE

Copyright © 2011 by HelenKay Dimon

ABOUT THE AUTHOR

Award-winning author HelenKay Dimon spent twelve years in the most unromantic career ever—divorce lawyer. After dedicating all that effort to helping people terminate relationships, she is thrilled to deal in happy endings and write romance novels for a living. Now her days are filled with gardening, writing, reading and spending time with her family in and around San Diego. HelenKay loves hearing from readers, so stop by her website at www.helenkaydimon.com and say hello.

Books by HelenKay Dimon

HARLEQUIN INTRIGUE
1196—UNDER THE GUN*
1214—NIGHT MOVES
1254—GUNS AND THE GIRL NEXT DOOR*
1260—GUNNING FOR TROUBLE*

*Mystery Men

CAST OF CHARACTERS

Caleb Mattern—This undercover Recovery Project agent is trying to adjust to involuntary retirement. Having his ex-girlfriend and former boss break into his house changes everything.

Avery Walker—She once made a tough decision she thought was right but ended up losing Caleb. Now she needs his help…and wants another chance to win him back.

Trevor Walters—A highly regarded and very powerful businessman. On the surface he is well connected and plays by the rules. But looks can be deceiving.

Rod Lehman—The missing head of the Recovery Project. His off-the-books investigation into missing women in the Witness Security Program could cost all the Recovery agents their lives.

Russell Ambrose—One of the few people with inside information about the workings of witness protection. So why doesn't he know what's happening on his watch?

John Tate—An administrator in the Office of Enforcement Operations at the Justice Department. He decides who gets into witness protection and who doesn't. The question is about what else he knows.

Vince Ritter—Rod's former partner. Vince shows up, offering his help to the Recovery agents, but can he be trusted?

Luke Hathaway—The interim head of the Recovery Project. He has vowed to keep his team together, even if it means sending Avery away.

Chapter One

Caleb Mattern's watch vibrated against his nightstand. The second after the warning alarm went off and the green backlight flashed, he rolled off the mattress fully awake with his hand grabbing for the gun tucked between the bottom of the headboard and his stack of pillows.

Dressed only in a pair of gray boxer briefs, he reached for the watch and stalked in a crouch through his dark bedroom. The curtains were drawn tight, not letting any light seep in and ruin his nightly four hours of sleep. Any brightness and he wouldn't even get that much.

So, this is how the end would come. Trapped in a one-bedroom condo in his underwear. He smiled at the thought. Or he did until his fingers tightened on the weapon, causing his mind to snap to attention.

Being armed felt right. He could shoot, attack, roll. Do whatever was necessary to stay alive. He'd learned those skills long ago, and being on involuntary leave from the job he loved didn't change the adrenaline rush.

He stalked around the end of the bed, his feet quiet

as they fell against the soft beige carpet. Opening the door to the hall would be more of a challenge. He rigged it every night. If someone got into the place without triggering the alarm, he had backup plans: a loose floorboard just outside the bedroom; a window that opened only two inches before the sirens of hell rang out; a hinge rigged to squeak if the door opened.

And those were just the obvious tricks.

As fast as his fingers could move, he tightened the screw at the top of the door. At the right pressure it would remain silent and he could pull off a stealth maneuver into the hall. But too long in this position and any bullet traveling through the door would hit him right in the gut. Not exactly the way he wanted to go out of this world.

He pulled the door open enough to slip through. Quiet echoed all around him. Other than the low hum of the refrigerator down the hall, nothing else made a sound.

The place was about seven hundred square feet. He liked it small. Made it easier to strategize and attack if needed, and it looked as if tonight called for an ambush. If the intruder so much as breathed, Caleb would be all over him.

Easing into the hallway, he hesitated just long enough for his eyes to fully adjust to the dark. He stepped around the purposely creaky floorboard and headed down the short corridor to the open area. From there he could see every angle of the condo.

A shuffling noise sounded in front of him. His gaze swept over the family room and into the small kitchen area on his left.

Nothing.

Well, nothing at eye level. A quick survey of the floor told him what he needed to know. Not that he could see the intruder. But the guy had made a mistake. The slimmest edge of a canvas bag stuck out from behind the couch. Could be a trap but there were only a few places for someone to spring up from behind Caleb. He had his ankle wedged against the laundry door just in case someone managed to curl up in there and hide. That left the few feet of space between the couch and the television.

The rat-a-tat drumming of energy pounded through Caleb. He didn't waste one more second waiting to get shot first. He ducked down, using the piece of furniture as a shield. Him on one side and the target on the other. In one smooth move, he launched his body up over the top of the sofa. The first grab turned up only air. He stretched forward on the second lunge, saw a flash of brown hair and then grabbed a shirt collar and pulled back. Caleb shoved his gun into the intruder's temple just as the screaming started.

He was a she. A very pissed-off she.

Arms and legs thrashed. Books from his coffee table fell to the floor as she kicked out, missing the television by inches. Fingernails scraped against his forearm. When she bit him, he shoved her away. She lost her balance, careening right for the plasma screen but she caught herself in time. She spun around, her eyes wide with shock, chest rising and falling in a rhythm guaranteed to bring on a heart attack.

Identifying the threat almost did it for him. It was as if the blood stammered to a halt in his veins. "Avery?"

"Caleb?"

His muscles burned from the quick diversion from the fight. "Uh, yeah."

"Why are you sneaking around?"

Avery Walker, former boss and lover. She fired him exactly two years ago next month. He dumped her right after. They'd carefully avoided each other ever since. "That's my question. It's four in the morning."

"I know."

"And how did you get into my house?"

"I can explain."

His breathing finally pulled back to near-normal levels. "You bet you will. And while you're at it, tell me what you're doing here."

"I came to talk to you."

"There's this new invention called the telephone." He took in her tight mouth and the white-knuckle grip on the side of his television. "What's wrong with you?"

"Could you lower the gun?"

Out of habit it was still aimed right for her heart. He dropped his arm to his side but didn't put the weapon away. Not until he knew what was going on. "Better?"

"Barely."

He felt the same way. Seeing her ripped through his usual wall of control. The jeans and bulky sweater seemed out of place for someone who spent most of her life in a lab coat. Studying her, he saw the same long brown hair and the huge dark eyes that could drop a man to his knees. She had just turned thirty-four, two years older than him, yet her round face and smooth skin made her look a good ten years younger.

The off-the-charts hotness factor had also made some of her days at Hancock Labs tough. Men talked down to her while they ogled her hourglass figure and tight butt. There were few women there, but the one near the top of the food chain piled menial jobs on top of Avery's heavy workload as a DNA analyst, as if daring her to fail.

Caleb knew because he watched it all play out. Quietly fought battles on Avery's behalf without her knowledge. Then she got promoted, the rumors started and everything fell apart.

"You can let go of my television now." They had enough bad blood between them without adding a couple of thousand dollars' worth of smashed electronics.

"It's not what you think."

He actually had no idea what to think. "Okay."

"This is an emergency."

He stared at his front door, but didn't see any sign of a break-in. "How did you get on this side of the door?"

Her arms slowly fell to her sides as she blew out a long breath. "You ask a lot of questions."

"Try answering any of them. Just pick one and start talking"

"I used the code and this to get in." She slipped her fingers into her jeans pocket and pulled out a shiny key.

The move stunned him more than seeing her face. "I didn't live here when we...before...so you sure shouldn't know my code, though I'm thinking you have an old one since my alarm still went off. And don't try to tell me I gave you a key, because we both know that's not true."

Her chin lifted. "Not to this or any other apartment."

"Is now the right time for that discussion?"

She threw the key on the couch cushion between them. "You're the one who's been running. Not me."

He refused to take the bait. "So, you decided burglary was the best way to get my attention?"

"Forget that." She waved her hands in front of her. "I'm not here about us."

The fact she could dismiss their relationship now as easily as she did two years ago sent his temperature spiking. Had his hand squeezing against the gun until the metal dug into his skin. "What else is there?"

"I had to find you."

"Why?"

"Rod told me if he ever…"

"Stop." Caleb stepped around the sofa to stand in front of her. "Rod who?"

She didn't roll her eyes, but she looked as though she wanted to. "The man you work for. Rod Lehman."

With his free hand, Caleb wrapped his fingers around her elbow and dragged her even closer, his chest practically resting against hers. He dropped his voice to a whisper just to be safe. "You can't know about this."

"About the Recovery Project? About your undercover work?" She tried to wiggle free, but he didn't ease his grip. "I assure you, I know."

"Not possible."

She flattened her palm against his chest, her gaze searching his face as she talked. "Caleb, listen to what I'm telling you."

The soft touch of her hand burned through him. The feel of skin against skin lit his nerve endings on fire. It had always been that way with her. Despite the fury and betrayal, his body reacted to her nearness.

He stepped back to break the hold, physical and otherwise, she had over him. "This is nuts."

"We don't have a lot of time."

"For what?"

She bent down and grabbed her bag. "I have information for Rod. Where is he?"

Nothing she said made any sense. The Recovery Project was top secret, an off-the-books, quasi-governmental agency that hunted missing people, both those who wanted to stay missing and those who wanted to be found. Or it was until a congressman with a personal vendetta pulled the funding and disbanded the group. Now it functioned as a private, rogue investigative organization.

Rod had always spearheaded Recovery, handpicked its operatives, but he had nothing to do with Caleb's past. And Avery was most certainly his past. "What do you know about Rod?"

"Like I said, he's your boss."

Caleb wanted to shake her, but touching her again was out of the question. "Damn it, Avery. That's not public information, and I think you know it."

"He told me if I needed him and couldn't find him through our usual communication channels—"

"What does that mean?"

"I should come to you." She sent Caleb that disapproving frown, complete with flat-lined lips. The same look he dredged up from memory whenever he got dangerously close to calling her to talk over old times. Caleb shook his head. "So?"

"I don't know where he is."

She went from frowning to sighing, another of her annoying specialties. "This isn't the time to play super-secretive-operative guy. Rod told me if he ever failed to check in, I should come to you. So, here I am."

She talked as if she worked for Rod, but that was impossible. Rod was his boss. The man ran Recovery, or he did until he disappeared, leaving behind only cryptic notes about a problem in the Witness Security Program, WitSec.

Caleb shook his head as he tried to make sense of his colliding worlds. "We're starting this conversation over."

"No, we're not." She pulled her bag over her shoulder as she looked him up and down. "Go get dressed. I have to keep moving."

"Why?" Caleb barely got the word out when he heard the scraping at the front door. He expected reinforcements, but not from that direction. "Did you relock it?"

"Of course."

A danger signal flashed in Caleb's brain. He grabbed Avery by the wrist and pulled her into the small kitchen while the panel on his watch went wild with racing lights. His stare never wavered from the door. He raised the weapon with one hand and reached around Avery to unlock the window behind her with the other.

"Out on the fire escape and then go down. Do not wait or stop until I tell you." He whispered the command right as the front door shattered off its hinges.

Wood splintered and cracked. A metallic smell mixed with a puff of gray smoke. The too-late alarm screeched inside his condo while the building's fire alarm kicked to life out in the hall. A gun barrel peeked into the room as the door across the hall opened, only to slam shut again.

Caleb didn't wait. He turned to the empty space beside him, relieved to see Avery gone, and then slipped out the window. As quiet as possible, he closed the glass behind him. Ignoring the cold air against his bare skin, he started crawling down the metal steps. His feet touching against the cold, he was careful not to slip or make noise to draw the gunman's attention. Caleb counted on the guy searching the bedroom first. That would be the instinct, to go into the other room, which was exactly why Caleb's escape route didn't lead that way.

Police sirens wailed in the distance as the lights flickered and the building came alive with activity. Avery was a floor below him. She kept glancing up but never stopped moving. When she hit the landing two floors down, he banged the gun against the metal railing to get her attention.

She stopped and shrugged her shoulders at him. Only Avery could maintain her offended sense of bossiness in the midst of a crisis.

Some neighbors flooded into the street as others

ducked their heads out windows, looking for the source of the noise and confusion. The action made sneaking away to safety even more difficult. Skipping the last few steps, Caleb jumped down, landing on the platform beside Avery and ignoring the feel of whatever was underneath him.

"Why are we stopping?" she asked.

He didn't take the time to explain. With his hand on her shoulder, he moved her to the side and slipped his fingers between the sill and wall of the window two floors below his condo.

She slapped at his arm. "What if the people are home?"

With a touch of his watch he silenced the alarm for this condo before it could go off and join the others. The window lock clicked open and he raised the glass. "They're not."

"You can't know that."

"I own this, too. It's my escape route." He glanced around but all attention seemed centered on the lobby and the two fire engines pulling up to the curb, instead of the guy in his underwear on the steps.

"Well, of course you own it." She sat on the frame and then swung her legs inside. "Doesn't everyone keep two condos in the same building?"

"I don't remember you being this sarcastic this early in the morning when we dated."

"At this time of the day sarcasm is all I *can* manage." She continued to grumble even as he followed her inside.

"You could try being grateful that I had a contingency plan."

She stood in the middle of the studio apartment. "Is there a light switch?"

So much for gratitude. "Leave it off for now. The only thing in here is a couch, so you don't need to worry about tripping and I don't want you skulking around anyway."

He walked past her and headed for the front door, trying to block out the emergency evacuation message blaring through the building on an endless loop. The speakers were mounted in the hall, but the beeping followed by the monotone voice instructing occupants to use the stairs and meet in the lobby echoed all through his small space. He'd hear that thundering warning in his sleep. That was, if he ever had the chance to sleep again.

Looking through the peephole, he saw people scurrying in the hallway. Another neighbor simply opened his door, glanced out and then went back inside again. Caleb didn't care what anyone else did so long as no one tried to come inside.

He reached for his cell and remembered he wasn't wearing anything more than his underwear. No shoes. No shirt. Certainly no pockets.

"Do you have your phone?" he asked.

When Avery didn't answer, he turned around. She wasn't there.

Chapter Two

Avery felt a rush of air behind her right before a hand clamped over her mouth and another slipped around her waist, banding her arms to her sides. A startled scream died in her throat as she was dragged out of the room and deeper into the shadows. The fog cleared from her head just as panic bubbled up from her stomach.

The bare forearm and stone wall of a chest gave away the sex of her attacker. A man. A big man with a grip destined to leave indents on her skin. She kicked out her leg only to have his wrap around hers and lock it back. Her neck straining, she tried to get out a mumble over the shrieking building alarm, anything to warn Caleb.

"Avery, I asked you…" Caleb's comment faded as he scanned the room and his gaze fell on them. He reached for the switch and the overhead light flickered on.

Despite having her chest compressed and her jaw locked shut by some animal's fingers, her nerves stopped jumping around. Hearing Caleb's voice didn't send her spinning with relief, but it did bring back hope for survival. She knew him as a man who worked in a lab. This side of him, the part that felt at home with a gun and confident while engaging predators, was new to her, even though she always sensed that protective streak lurking beneath everything else. Heck, he didn't even let the fact he was half-naked stop him.

"Let her go." He didn't yell or threaten. Didn't even raise his weapon.

And that fast, the suffocating hold was gone. Off balance, she listed to the side only to have the attacker's hand return again, this time to steady her. But it was too late for calm. If Caleb wasn't going to shoot this guy, she would try to take him down. She turned and raised a fist to knock him into the fridge.

The attacker caught her clenched hand in his but didn't hurt her. "I don't think so," he said.

She tried to think of another way to cause damage. "Who are you?"

"The cavalry." The man's amused tone didn't match the black commando T-shirt or stealth attack. Then again, neither did the boyish dimple or the wire-rimmed glasses.

"He's with me." The second Caleb stepped up, the other man dropped her hand. The building alarm shut off right after.

"Thank God. I can hear again." The man nodded in Caleb's direction. "Nice outfit, by the way."

Avery followed the stare as she tried to calm her breathing. Looking at the muscles stretching across Caleb's bare chest sure didn't help with that task. He hadn't gotten soft in their years apart. If anything, he'd gotten more fit. She imagined this is what his body looked like back at the Naval Academy and in the years in the military that followed. There wasn't an ounce of fat on his stomach.

Those broad shoulders brought back memories. They would lie in bed with him hovering over her. She used to love to run her fingers over his skin, dip into the space between his collarbone and his neck, and then up and through his sandy brown hair. The man possessed the sexiest green-gray eyes she had ever seen.

And a stubborn streak that made her head pound.

"You got here fast," Caleb said to the man who was obviously a friend and not an enemy.

"Always nice when a contingency plan works," the man said as he stole glances in her direction.

When Caleb didn't explain what was happening or even bother to act like standing there half-naked after his front door exploded was an odd thing, she took the lead. The way she figured it, she'd tolerated just about enough confusion for one evening. If her heart raced any faster, she was going to pass out. Last thing she needed was the show of male bonding, not with armed guys hunting for them only a few floors above.

She looked up at the stranger. Caleb stood about six feet, but this guy had to be another three or so inches taller, so looking up was her only option. "Who are you?"

Caleb placed a hand against the small of her back. "Avery Walker, this is Adam Wright. We work together."

Adam nodded his head. "Ma'am."

"You don't want to know why I'm with Caleb?"

She saw Adam swallow back a smile. "I figure if

you're here, it's because he wants you to be. The rest isn't my business."

"He's the computer genius of the group," Caleb said, cutting through the personal stuff.

Adam scowled at Caleb but he missed it and Avery was too busy fighting off the flood of anger pouring through her. "Computers? Are you kidding? Felt more like you were the pain enforcer to me. You scared the he—"

Adam held up his hands as if surrendering, even though he held a gun in one. "And you were a worthy adversary. If I hadn't stopped you just then, we'd be picking my teeth up off the floor."

"We still might," she mumbled.

Adam smiled. "Fair enough."

She refused to be charmed or put off. Concentrating while Caleb stood there in his tight underwear was hard enough. "Anyone want to tell me what's going on?"

"Adam is with Recovery."

Adam's shoulders tensed. "Caleb, what are you—"

"She knows."

Adam looked back and forth between Caleb and Avery. "Not possible."

The poor guy looked ready to vomit, which she figured served him right after the squeeze play he put on her midsection. "Totally possible."

Caleb blew out a long, exaggerated breath. "Apparently it is."

She saw Adam's hand shift toward his gun. She saw it and Caleb saw it.

"Stop." Caleb pressed his hands down as if trying

to calm the situation. "Avery is safe. Trust me. I'm not worried about her alliances."

She had no idea what that meant but the whole talking-like-she-wasn't-there thing wasn't her favorite.

"She does about Rod and Recovery." She hesitated to make sure her sarcasm made an impression. "My question was really about why we're in this condo and when exactly Caleb here had the time to call in the cavalry here."

He had the nerve to shrug. "We all have contingency plans in case of an emergency."

"I'm his," Adam said.

They acted as if that explained everything. "I still don't get it."

"If the silent alarm trips—" Adam pointed to his watch as he spoke "—I come running. If Caleb isn't here or on that fire escape, I know he needs help."

"You got here before we did."

"I live in the building and was already in the condo when the building's fire alarm started blaring. Something tripped Caleb's silent alarm before that."

"You mean someone." Caleb played with the buttons on his watch, as if the conversation bored him. "Avery broke into my apartment."

"Impressive." Adam's tone and his slow nod suggested he meant it.

Caleb finally looked up again. "And now we're stuck because there are police and bad guys roaming around, and I'm not sure which is which."

"Do we know the identity of said bad guys?" Adam asked. "Just wondering who we ticked off this time."

As much as she wanted to hear about whatever idiot would be self-destructive enough to come after these two, she jumped in. "You didn't. I did."

She waited until both men looked at her. She wanted to make sure she had their attention because she needed them to understand how serious the situation had become. "They want me."

Caleb stared at her for a few seconds without saying anything. Then he wrapped his fingers around her elbow and turned toward the front door. "Then despite the danger, we have to get you out of here and somewhere safe."

"You might want to put on some clothes first," Adam called out, right before she could.

Caleb stopped in midstep and glanced down his front. "Good plan."

Adam shook his head. "I'll get them."

She waited until Adam stepped into the bathroom to whisper her question to Caleb. "Can he be trusted?"

He stared after Adam, glanced around the room, basically did everything but give her the courtesy of looking at her. "Yeah. Adam's one of the few people I do trust."

There was nothing subtle in Caleb's comment. "Unlike me?"

This time his gaze locked on hers. "Yeah, Avery. Unlike you."

TREVOR WALTERS LEANED back in his oversize leather chair and stared at the men sitting on the other side of his desk. They were experts in their fields but he could control them both with a few phone calls, as evidenced by the fact they showed up on his turf before five in the morning, before the workday even started. Likely before these government workers normally woke up. They asked for a meeting. He set the unreasonable terms to see if they'd meet them. Not a surprise they had.

His company, Orion Industries, specialized in threat management. He advised governments and corporations, supplying assessments and muscle. Today his country's government had come calling in the form of a fifty-something bureaucrat with graying hair, a runner's build and a Georgetown Law class ring.

"We're here on a sensitive subject," John Tate said, then stopped. It was as if he thought his impressive title at the Department of Justice gave him the right to make demands.

Trevor wasn't impressed by the deputy director of the Office of Enforcement Operations. The man oversaw complex surveillance and witness protection requests, including who got in and who didn't. But with all that power the guy still had no clue about the corruption raging through his office.

Russell Ambrose, the other man in the room, knew all about deceit. As chief inspector in the D.C. office of WitSec and a career government official with the U.S. Marshal Service, he should have been crystal clean. Trevor knew from experience that wasn't the case.

Trevor knew. Russell knew. Tate, the man at the very top, was the only one in the dark. Trevor almost smiled at the irony.

"You know I am always willing to lend my company's services if needed," he said.

John gave a quick glance in Russell's direction before starting. "I'm afraid this is a bit more personal."

Trevor had an idea where the conversation was headed but wanted to make the man spell it out. Let John squirm a bit. In Trevor's view, powerful men always did the best squirming. "How so?"

"Your brother." John brushed lint or something equally invisible off his pants. "I'm very sorry for your loss, by the way."

"Thank you."

"I attended the service. It was very moving."

"Agreed." Trevor had planned it, headed the cover-up into the true cause of the death and saw to it everyone believed his brother died a hero. Their parents deserved to grieve with honor. Having the world view Bram as the model statesman and father served that purpose. It also ensured a steady stream of contracts for Trevor's company. Bram got the praise and Trevor reaped the benefits. He could live with the deal, even though the sting of Bram's loss pricked stronger than Trevor expected it would.

In the quiet of his home office with only his whiskey as witness, he had mourned. He'd let the weakness flow through him. Mostly, though, he simmered with fury that Bram had gotten pulled so far into the terrible situation that led to his murder. He had been so reckless and paid the ultimate price.

Russell tapped the thin file resting on his lap. "We need some information."

"You should know I don't have any access to Bram's records. Those were in his congressional office and are confidential." Except for the boxes Trevor had already destroyed. He had owed Bram that much. Preserve his memory and bury the evidence. That had always been their unspoken deal if the worst happened.

John nodded. "Of course, but—"

Trevor flipped through his Rolodex even though he knew the number by heart. "Bram's former chief of staff, David Brennan, is handling everything in the office pending a special election to fill Bram's seat. David is one of the nominees and the likely successor. You can call him to get what you need."

John put out his hand as if to stop Trevor's movements. "This relates to work outside Bram's job as U.S. Representative."

"Former."

"What?"

"My brother died saving a member of his office staff." The kidnapping of Mia Landers by her abusive ex, the shoot-out, the inevitable death toll even Trevor could not hide. It all played out exactly as Bram had planned, except for where he got caught in the cross fire. That had been a possibility, but a remote one. "As such, my brother is no longer a member of Congress. Or of anything else, for that matter."

At least that was the carefully constructed story Trevor had sold to the world with the cooperation of the Recovery Project agents, the very men who killed Bram.

John's squirming started right as expected. "Yes, well, I am aware of that."

"Then you also know my brother and I kept our respective careers separate. Since I deal in government contracts, it would have been a conflict of interest for Bram to be involved in my business and vice versa."

"I'm sorry to hear that," John said under his breath.

"Why?"

Russell opened the mysterious file in front of him. "We have some questions relating to the congressman's role in the Witness Security Program."

"Witness protection? Isn't that your specialty? Both of you." Trevor let his gaze travel over the two men, hesitating just long enough to make sure they understood who controlled this conversation.

Trevor knew Russell wrongly believed he had the upper hand. His attempts at blackmail had proved that much. Trevor admitted to the serious miscalculation in letting Russell worm his way into his private life. Trevor vowed never to make that mistake again.

"It would seem your brother also had an interest in WitSec. He made several inquiries prior to his death, some through proper channels and others not," Russell said.

Trevor had warned Bram not to dig, or at least to be careful when he did. One of his brother's many failures had been his oversize ego and naive belief that his office would protect him no matter how egregious the offense. Trevor knew better. He had seen dictators of small countries fall, even helped make it happen, so he understood the devastating impact of poor choices and emotional thinking.

"I'm afraid I can't help you," he said.

John shifted to the front part of his chair. "Is it possible the congressman sought information about witness protection on your behalf?"

"No."

"You're sure?"

"Quite."

John frowned. "Yet you're not offended by my question."

"You learn many things when you lose a sibling. You understand that no matter what you've achieved in this world or how much power you command, some things remain out of your final control." Trevor leaned back in his chair. "Except my temper. It would seem that is the one thing I can control."

Russell closed his file without ever reading a word from it. "Maybe if we looked through your correspondence we might see something you didn't."

"That is not possible, as I'm sure you know. Not with the confidential nature of my work. I have clients, and their needs must be protected." But now Trevor knew the real reason for the visit. They wanted free access. John suspected him, of what wasn't clear, but Trevor knew the groundwork once laid could be a significant problem.

"I was hoping to handle this privately," John said.

"I believe we just did." Trevor stood up and tugged on the bottom of his suit jacket to make sure it had fallen back in place. "Now, if that's all, gentlemen?"

Russell took the hint and rose to his feet. "Of course. We won't take any more of your time."

Trevor had to bite back a wave of bile whenever he

looked at Russell. He was the worst kind of man—one dripping in weakness who wrongly believed he possessed strength.

He paid Russell well to make sure meetings like this never happened. Looked like the man needed a reminder of the terms of their deal. "Nonsense. I am always available to government officials."

"We do all want the same thing here," John said.

Trevor seriously doubted that. "And what would that be?"

"Justice." Russell fumbled over the word. Not a surprise since as far as Trevor could tell the man did not have any concept of the word.

"I've always found that term somewhat elusive. After all, we don't all agree on what's just, now do we?" Trevor let the words sink in before he headed for the door to show them out.

John hesitated for a second but then followed. "If you think of anything, you will let us know, correct?"

"Of course."

Russell nodded. "We would appreciate that."

Trevor decided Russell would do more than that. He would have a front-row seat to what happened next. "Rest assured I will do everything necessary to resolve our issues."

Chapter Three

They climbed down the fire escape on the outside of the building, Adam behind her and Caleb in front. Caleb tried to think of another way to hide Avery, but he suspected her pursuers would start going door to door and keep coming. That meant they had to get out and away as fast as possible. Since there were police cars and fire trucks downstairs, their options were limited. Almost nonexistent, actually.

"Where are we going?" Avery asked as she carefully placed her feet on the metal rungs.

"Anywhere but here."

She shot him a frown over her shoulder. "Am I supposed to know what that means?"

"No."

She stopped ten steps up from the street and stared up at him. "You could try answering the question without being a jerk."

He knew he should, but something about her brought out the worst in him. So did being woken up in the middle of the night to go running all over his condo building, dodging men with guns. "You're the one being followed."

"Because of Rod." Her knuckles turned white where they held the strap to her shoulder bag. Any tighter and she'd cut off circulation.

Adam popped up next to her. "Uh, kids. I get that you two have some history and all, and I want to hear about it, I do, but we need to keep moving."

Caleb heard the warning behind his friend's joking tone and heeded it. "Right. We can fight about this later. Preferably when we're out of earshot of anyone holding a weapon."

"Fine." She sounded anything but.

"Fine."

Adam nodded. "Happy to hear we're all fine. So, can we get moving?"

"One question." Avery pointed at the side of the building. "There are cameras all over the place. Won't the attackers look for us and then follow?"

"I cut their access," Adam said. "Anyone checking the security monitors is seeing an endless loop of barren hallways and quiet outdoor areas."

Caleb clicked the bottom button on his watch and showed her Adam's tech handiwork. "See? There's nothing on there that can help them or hurt us."

Adam tapped a finger against his forehead. "Computer genius."

"But, when did you manage to do all of that?" she asked.

"I set up the program the day we moved in and check it every week to make sure I'm still dialed in and can take over if needed. When the silent alarm went off, I switched the security monitors to my loop and have been sending the real footage to my off-site computer so I can analyze it later. The only potential problem is that the police will check it and know someone tampered with it."

"You?"

"Oh, they won't trace it back to me."

She smiled for the first time all evening. "I guess you can do more than grab women and scare the crap out of them."

"Since I'm not sure how to answer that, I won't," Adam said.

Caleb had had enough conversation. He wasn't too fond of Avery's reaction to Adam either. Hearing them joke back and forth while he stood right there was not Caleb's idea of a good time. It made him want to punch something. Like Adam.

Leave it to Avery to come between them. From his experience, she ruined everything. Seemed she hadn't lost that trait.

But they had a bigger problem at the moment and it—or rather, they—had just turned the corner and were heading down the alley. When Adam tensed, Caleb figured his friend had seen them, too. It took Avery a little longer, but her sharp intake of breath signaled her awareness.

"Everything okay up there?" The policeman was on top of them in a few steps. He put his hand on his gun and his partner beside him followed suit.

Two men in their late forties, if Caleb had to guess.

Uniforms, matching battle stances, calm tone. Caleb wasn't getting the paid-assassin vibe from them, but he inched his fingers closer to the weapon tucked in his waistband just in case. He noticed Adam did the same.

Caleb decided to play dumb until one of their guests gave him a reason to start shooting. "Is it a fire? If so, we figured it wasn't safe to use the elevators."

"Something like that." The officer's shoulders relaxed. "You see anyone else wandering around over here or upstairs?"

Avery shook her head, but the rest of her body remained rock still. "No, sir."

The officer motioned them off the steps. "Then get moving. You should have been out and on the street a half hour ago."

"We thought it was a drill."

The officers waited until the three of them stepped on the macadam. "We need everyone out until we confirm the electrical fire and make sure it's under control. Can you three find your way?"

Even though they looked to be in the clear, Caleb didn't let any of the tension leave his body. He stayed ready. "Absolutely."

The officer nodded. "Get moving."

They waited until the police turned the corner to the front of the building again before anyone said anything. Finally, Avery let out a shaky breath. "That was close."

"Too much so." They kept to the side of the brick wall, out in the alley and far out of the line of sight of any of the professionals or gunmen who may be walking around the front of the complex as Caleb explained their plan. "Adam will act as a decoy and drive Avery's car. We'll take his alternate truck and head in the opposite direction."

"Alternate what? You know what? Forget it. I'm not going to ask." Avery reached into her bag and grabbed her keys. "Here. I'm parked on the street."

Adam took them and then threw his set to Caleb. "I'm in the garage."

Caleb felt more faith in the plan than he did five seconds ago. "Even better. We can divert their attention."

"But there are people everywhere." Her wild-eyed gaze traveled between the men. "And then there's the part where this is dangerous. Adam could be hurt."

"We could all be killed." Caleb took in her open-mouthed stare and decided she still didn't get it. "What did you think was supposed to happen when my front door exploded? That wasn't a friendly hello."

A fiery heat replaced the worry in her eyes. "I am well aware of what happened, Caleb. I was there."

"They broke into my house with weapons drawn. They, whoever they are—and you will be filling me in on that as soon as I get you to safety—were not there to talk."

As a result, his condo, her house and anywhere else obvious was out as a hiding place.

That left the new Recovery Project headquarters as their option. The place was little more than an empty shell, an abandoned warehouse, but it couldn't be traced to her and that's all that mattered at the moment.

"You can stop talking to me like I'm an idiot."

Oh, he knew she wasn't that. She was smart and confident and driven. He'd lost his last job thanks to her and her ambitions. "Their orders likely were to grab you, kill me and take you somewhere for questioning. That means torture, Avery. You do understand, right?"

Adam shoved at Caleb's shoulder. "Ease up."

"She needs to understand."

"I think she does."

She stepped in front of Adam and right up to Caleb's chest. "I'm sorry I involved you. Is that what you want to hear?"

Seeing her clenched fists and pale face knocked the temper right out of him. "If you're right, you didn't. Rod did."

"He couldn't have anticipated putting you in danger," she asked.

"That's exactly what he thought would happen." Caleb tried to shut off his questions about Rod and WitSec and every other disaster, and focus instead on the problem in front of him. "Avery, that's what we do."

"This?"

"Exactly this."

She hesitated a second more. "Then it's good I'm with you."

Them. Together. Caleb had to block out those images. "We'll see if you feel that way in a half hour."

"What happens then?"

"We'll know if we escaped without gunfire," Adam said and then turned to Caleb. "The truck is in my extra space on the top floor. No one will be looking for it or put me together with Avery. Keep her head down until you're away, just to be safe. Don't stop for any reason—roadblocks, questioning, I don't care. If I need to cause a scene on my end to get you out, I will."

"Sounds like you guys have done this before." Her nervous laugh ruined her attempt at a joke.

"We've done far worse," Caleb said.

Adam winked at her. "Certainly far stranger."

"I'm driving a red sedan. I don't know the license plate, so you'll have to hit the automatic locks if there's more than one of that color." Her hand shook as she brushed her hair off her face. "It's up the street on the left."

One piece of information didn't mesh with what Caleb knew about Avery. "Why don't you know your license plate?"

"It's my neighbor's car."

"Does she know you have it?"

"He doesn't. I took it without asking."

Caleb pushed the male reference out of his mind. They didn't date anymore. She could see anyone she wanted and it wasn't his business. He repeated the comment in his head three times, and the reality still refused to sink in. The idea of her with someone else made his back teeth slam together.

"With our luck the guy reported it and Adam will get picked up for stealing it," Caleb grumbled, more at the idea of the neighbor than anything else.

She reached out and touched his arm. "My point is that the bad guys shouldn't recognize the car, so Adam should skip the driving around part and come with us."

"Negative." Caleb made the comment right as Adam started shaking his head.

She dropped her hand back to her side. "Both of you?"

"It's a safety measure," Adam explained.

"And we're done talking." Caleb gave his command and then turned to Adam. "Head for the street. If the situation is too hot, ping me, keep walking and I'll send someone to come around to pick you up."

"Someone?" she asked.

"Another agent." Caleb wondered if she thought he and Adam worked alone.

Her mouth dropped open. "How many more of you are there?"

Adam chuckled. "Three. Does that scare you?"

The shock turned into a small smile. "The exact opposite, actually."

"Let's go." Caleb slipped his hand under her elbow and used his key to open the outside door to the garage.

Chapter Four

To anyone watching they might have looked like a loving couple. In reality, Caleb had a death grip on her skin as he pulled her out and onto the underground garage floor. If he thought she would run, he was wrong. She was too busy trying to keep her dinner in her stomach rather than on the cement in front of her. The internal muscles heaved and rumbled. Everything sloshed and moved.

She'd never had a run-in with the police. Never had men track her down, or seen a door explode either. Car chases and gunfire—if this was Caleb's life now, she almost felt bad for firing him. He had been insubordinate and difficult, rarely followed the rules and liked to solve cases instead of limit his work to DNA testing, but he was safe there. So was she. A few more minutes of this level of panic and she was going to throw up. Or worse.

Caleb scanned the large open floor from one end of the cement block area to the other. It didn't take long, since the floor consisted of four rows of cars separated by two lanes. There was an elevator and a guard cubicle where the cars entered and left but it appeared empty, as opposed to most of the parking spaces. They were full.

"Where is everyone?" she asked.

"Probably up on the street."

His gaze stopped searching and fell on her. "You're turning green."

"I'm terrified." Her teeth rattled to prove it.

"I've never known you to be scared of anything."

"I could make a comment about you not knowing me at all, but now probably isn't the right time."

A sharp honk of a horn grabbed his attention, but when the car pulled out and left the garage he stared back down at her. "You think?"

"Believe it or not, I'm not a complete idiot."

"Never said you were. Never thought it either." His gaze flashed over her shoulder for the briefest of moments as he hurried their steps to a parking spot near the stairwell.

She would have missed his look if she hadn't been concentrating on the unique mix of green and gray in his eyes in an effort not to double over. "What is it?"

"There's a guy to our far right, standing just inside the garage door exit. Pretend to cough and give a quick peek over at him. Ready?"

"Yeah." She concentrated, making sure to keep her head down as she did what he asked.

"Look familiar?"

"Not at all."

"Did you see the guys who were following you?" Caleb aimed the key chain at the small black truck as he whispered his question. The click echoed through the floor as the automatic locks opened.

"I didn't know anyone was behind me until your front door caved in."

He opened the truck door for her. "Put the seat belt on and then lean down as if you're checking in the glove compartment. I want your head out of shooting range."

"Does this thing have air bags?"

"Adam took them out just for this type of situation."

She thought it made more sense to load the truck with them. "Why?"

"You'd smother if we got hit."

"You're not making me feel very confident."

"Right now my job is to keep you alive. We'll worry about how happy you are later." He walked around to his side and slid in. He jammed the key in the ignition as he strapped the belt across his lap and put the shoulder strap behind him.

"What about your head?"

"I'm going to need it to drive."

"That's comforting."

"See, I'm getting better at the making-you-feel-confident thing already."

She wanted to snort, but she followed his orders instead. Well, most of them. The not-moving part proved impossible as she glanced over the dashboard. The sight in front of her sent fear whirling through every cell and muscle. The man who stood around smoking a cigarette earlier now ran toward them, his face red and his arms pumping. "The guy is moving."

"I see him." Caleb pressed a hand against her shoulder and pushed her cheek closer to the leather seat. "No matter what you hear, stay down."

"Why?" Footsteps thundered closer. A deep voice shouted for them to stop.

"He's aiming his gun." Caleb ducked even as he sent the truck flying out of its spot and screeching into the lane. "Down!"

Gunfire rang out all around them. Loud pings sounded as the bullets hit metal. She crouched into a tight ball and pressed as close to Caleb's thigh as the seat belt digging into her thigh would allow. The smell of heated rubber stung her nose as the vehicle lurched forward then picked up speed. Tires squealing, they headed in the general direction of the exit.

Before they had gone ten feet, an engine revved off to her right. At least she thought it was that side; at the awkward angle everything sounded muffled and distorted. This wasn't just someone pulling out. This was someone looking to ram them. She knew that as sure as she knew she'd never make it out of this situation without Caleb's help.

The whirl of tires grew louder, as if another vehicle were about to drive through her skull. She braced her elbow against the seat and touched the seat belt to make sure it was secure.

"Hold on." The back end of the truck spun around and smashed into something solid as a rush of air passed by them on the right side.

The jolt slammed her forward. Her skin burned from the strangling belt. The contents of her stomach raced up her throat as her eyes began to water.

He shot her a worried frown. "Okay?"

"Fine." She saw Caleb hit the gas, but the car didn't move. When he switched gears, she closed her eyes and said a little prayer that they would survive this nightmare. "Were we hit?"

"No."

"You're a target." With her hand tangled in his shirt, she tried to pull him out of the line of fire.

"Just stay down."

Caleb never stopped moving. The wheel shook under his iron grip as he shifted his position and swore. When he hit the gas this time, the car raced through the small space.

She could hear him screaming Adam's name, which didn't make any sense since he wasn't in the garage. With her eyes closed, she hunched there and waited for the truck's walls to cave in around her. She wanted to crawl onto the floor and sit with her hands over her head, pretending none of this was happening.

But she needed to know he was okay. "Caleb!"

"What?"

His sharp response actually felt good. Hope sprang up out of nowhere, tamping down the fear bubbling up inside of her.

"No matter what, do not sit up!" His voice lost the stiff tone he'd been using with her. He now sounded wild, out of control and yelling.

She had no intention of ignoring him on this. She

slid as close to him as possible. With her head tilted, she pulled her hair to the side so she could see what was happening above her.

"Hide your face." With his body flat against the steering wheel, Caleb reached up and touched something against the windshield. It shattered into hundreds of tiny blocks.

Someone screamed, and she was pretty sure the high-pitched wail came from her. "What did you—"

"Safety glass."

The glass tumbled over her. She put up her hands to block the shower of glass, but she could feel the pieces in her hair and lying all around her. She didn't even notice the gun on his lap until he grabbed it and put the muzzle through what was once the windshield. He fired two shots as he accelerated and crossed through the garage entrance and out into the dark night.

She heard the police sirens wind up as soon as Caleb turned right onto the street and sped away from the building. He didn't slow for the speed bump. The truck went airborne then landed with a clunk against the ground. Glass cubes crunched around her. She struggled up to one elbow and looked him over. No blood, just huge eyes and clenched hands.

Tension bounced off him in waves. Every muscle in his body seemed to be pulled tight and ready to snap. "Caleb?"

He kept checking the rearview mirror. "We have about one minute to pull this off."

"What?"

"The switch."

She had no idea what he was talking about. For a minute she worried he'd knocked his head in their big escape. "Maybe we should—"

"I'm going to turn into another garage. Adam will pull up and your job is to jump in his car."

"How does he know where we are?"

Caleb shook his wrist. "I told him."

"When?"

"He's been listening."

The answer popped into her head. The watch. That thing performed miracles, as far as she could tell. It linked them. Provided information. It could actually save them.

She sat up and glanced behind them. The sirens screamed through the quiet streets, but she didn't see the cars yet. She figured they must have had a small lead, one Caleb tried to use in some way.

"Are you hurt?" she asked.

"I'll be fine."

The stiff arms made her think he was prepared for another option. Not that she would let it happen. She refused to be the reason he got injured. Jumping back into his life had not been her idea, but she had to take responsibility for dropping this mess on his lap. "I'm not leaving you in this car."

His gaze shot to her then back to the road. "Yes, you are."

"I can't."

"You will and I'll be right behind you."

"Caleb." She laid her hand on his thigh and felt the tight muscles jump underneath. "Keep driving."

"Not an option. Get ready." When she continued to sit there, he reached over and unsnapped her seat belt. "On my word you go."

She burned with the need to refuse. She wanted to stay with him, make sure he was safe and not in police hands—or worse. But the flat line of his mouth and flashing fire in his eyes told her to listen. Smart women didn't question a rescue when the plan for one landed in front of them.

"Avery?"

"Okay, okay." Not sure if he even intended to stop to let her out, she shifted. Crowding her body against the door, she was ready to move on his order.

"Remember your bag."

She'd forgotten all about it. When she arrived at his condo, it was the most important package in the world. The groundwork for Rod's concerns, everything she needed to make Caleb believe her, sat in there. Now surviving and making sure Caleb did also trumped all else.

The street sped by her as Caleb maneuvered through alleys and off main streets. Red lights switched to green as soon as he got near them. When he didn't bother to even tap the brakes to slow down, she figured Adam was providing access with another one of his computer programs. Assisted or not, Caleb managed to make a four-thousand-pound truck seem invisible on the abandoned streets.

He no longer hunched over the wheel. Shoulders back and eyes always moving, he drove fast and sure, like a man born to outrun the police.

He made a sharp turn that sent her flying into the door. "Sorry. We're almost there."

She could tell that by the noise. Sirens rang out in every direction. She half wondered if the entire police department had taken to their cars in pursuit.

"I'm ready," she said, even though she didn't feel it. Only now had her stomach stopped jumping around.

"Good."

She didn't even question his choice when he drove into a parking structure. She just slipped her fingers under the handle and waited to open the door. A glance over her shoulder at Caleb's firm jaw and steady determination made her heartbeat bounce in double time. She wanted to make him promise he'd be fine, but she knew that didn't matter to him. He was a warrior, strong and in charge, protective and dependable. Just as she always suspected.

Without warning he hit the brakes. "Go now."

Knowing seconds could mean the difference between him being safe and the absolute worst scenario, she didn't hesitate. She threw the door open just as her neighbor's car pulled up beside her, facing the opposite direction.

Adam held his arm out to her. "Get in."

They were men accustomed to having their commands followed. Not that she had any choice. The second she stepped out of the truck, Caleb had sped away. She could see the red brake lights and hear the tires squeal as he drove up the ramp to a higher floor of the garage.

"Avery, now."

"Right." She fell into the seat and dumped her bag on the floor.

By the time Adam pulled back out to the entrance of the garage, police cars had descended on the block. Two blew by them. Another pulled over and idled across the street.

"What's he doing?" She really wanted to know what they were doing just sitting there and why they hadn't left the area.

"Checking our plates."

"What?"

When the street cleared, Adam pulled out nice and slow. "That's what I would do if I were him."

"What if he stops us?"

"We're just a nice couple going home from a party. Lucky for us, our sobriety shouldn't be a problem."

"We're in the middle of a police chase."

"Innocent people get stuck in those all the time."

"Where exactly do you live that this sort of thing keeps happening near you and you have so much information on it?"

"Arlington, but you knew that, so I'll assume you're just engaging in a bit of nervous chatter." He checked the mirrors and then smiled over at her. "Your neighbor must have a clean driving record, because the officer isn't following us. Also, looks like your friend hasn't gotten up yet and realized the car's been stolen."

Her stomach turned again but for a very different reason this time. "I feel bad about that."

"Don't." Adam stole a quick look at her. "You did what you had to do and I'll return it."

Part of her knew that she hadn't had a choice, but she was too worried and panicked to think it through. "Where's Caleb?"

"You'll see in about two minutes." Amusement moved through Adam's voice.

"I thought I was the one with the nonsense-chatter problem."

"Nervous."

"What?"

"I said you had a problem with nerves." Adam pointed off to her right. "And there's Caleb. Standing on the corner right on time, as usual. Was he always this punctual?"

She glanced at the parking structure and the block between where they left Caleb and where they were now. "How did he—"

"Dumped the truck, ran down the stairs, circled around the building." Adam flashed her a smile. "You know, the usual."

"Impressive."

"Not really. That's the easy stuff."

"What's the hard stuff?"

"You don't want to know." Adam pulled over and unlocked the door. "Good to see you made it."

"Everything run according to plan?" Caleb asked as he climbed in the backseat.

"No issues."

"That's a first." He slumped back in his seat. "Head for the warehouse. Luke checked in. He's on his way there, so we'll have a welcoming party."

"Is it safe?" she asked as she turned around to face Caleb.

He sat with his gun resting on his knee and his attention focused on the scenery passing by outside the window. "It's totally secure. No one can get you there."

She wanted to knock the smugness right out of him. "I meant is it safe for us to drag a problem right to your friends' doorsteps."

"Of course."

A nasty reply died on her lips when she saw Caleb's drawn cheeks and the wrinkles at the corner of his eyes. "Are you okay?"

"Fine."

"You don't sound it."

"It's been a long night." When she scoffed, he focused those tired eyes on her. "I'll be great once I know what you have in that bag."

"Information." Almost everything they needed, and she hoped it was enough.

"And what is it you know that almost got us all killed?"

When he phrased it like that, it sucked the defensive anger right out of her. "I hope it's worth it."

"That makes two of us, Avery."

Chapter Five

Adam drove the car through the opened automatic gate and right into the warehouse garage by the southwest D.C. waterfront. When Avery stopped talking, Caleb assumed she was trying to take in her surroundings. He didn't blame her for the confusion. It didn't look like much.

From the outside it was just another broken-down beige building at the edge of a commercial warehouse district lined with broken-down beige buildings. An electrified fence outlined the lot. Huge floodlights burned, showing every inch of the property. Even without an obvious security guard, nothing about the place offered an inviting welcome.

The trucks that passed by on the way to load and unload merchandise at the other warehouses nearby accounted for most of the traffic in the area. Concrete walls and steel doors surrounded by cheap landscaping rocks and an empty parking lot were not exactly the usual signs of an intricate undercover operation. But that's what hid behind the walls—the start of the new Recovery Project headquarters.

Luke Hathaway had taken over running the Project in Rod's absence. His wife, Claire, thanks to an unwanted inheritance from her crooked ex-husband, gave them this new start. She didn't want anything from her ex, and she was all too happy to use the cash for something positive.

They got out of the car and headed for the huge door that separated the garages from the main hub of the organization. The cameras two stories above their heads swiveled to follow their movements just as the steel slab next to the door slid open to reveal a lighted panel.

"Impressive," Avery whispered.

"It will be in a few months." Caleb pressed his hand against the scanner. When the lights turned green, he tapped his watch against the screen.

"What happens then?"

"The office will be done." Caleb stepped back and waited for the thick door to push forward and roll open.

She stood at the threshold as if she worried stepping forward would set off a new set of alarms. "It looks pretty done right now."

Not even close. They had set up the security system, moved in the elaborate computer system and set up the rows of monitors and surveillance equipment Adam required. One whole wall flashed with buttons and images. There was a large conference table in the center of the L-shaped desks and screens.

The rest of the main floor was a work in progress, as was the loft at the top of the metal staircase that ran from the center of the room. Future plans included redoing the upstairs as a makeshift crash pad and building out the remainder for storage. A couch and relaxation area in the space under the stairs rounded out the blueprints.

Her gaze swept over the entire space. "So, this isn't your regular office?"

"It is now. We had a breach at the old one. Had to abandon it and find something new." Caleb left out the part where an assignment involving Claire blew their cover and accidentally invited the wrath of then-Congressman Bram Walters—now-dead Congressman Bram Walters. Recovery lost its office and legitimacy in the government's eyes. They'd been operating rogue ever since.

"Moving an office sounds worse than moving a house."

Adam snorted. "You wouldn't believe us if we tried to explain."

"We can actually go inside." Caleb whispered the suggestion in her ear. "Or are you afraid of getting shot at again?"

"Something like that."

Caleb put an end to her gawking. She was safe here and he wanted her to know that. With his hand on her lower back, he gently guided her into the main room. "I think we can all stand a drink and a chair."

Luke stepped in front of them, coffee cup in hand, wearing jeans and yawning. "Have a rough evening?"

"It must legitimately be morning by now," Adam mumbled.

"A little past six." Luke smiled at their guest. "I'm Luke Hathaway."

"Avery Walker." She barely moved her arm because she had a death hold on her bag but did shake his hand.

"Were you injured?" Luke asked.

"Just rattled. I'll be fine."

"Where is everyone else?" Caleb asked.

Luke took a long swallow of coffee. "Zach should be here in five minutes. Holden is at the house watching over Claire and Mia."

Avery didn't act as if she was even paying attention to the conversation. Her gaze went to the ceiling and the industrial lights and open beams. "Wait, did you say women work for you?"

Luke laughed. "I'm pretty sure Claire thinks we all work for her, but no. She's my wife. Mia is Holden's..." He looked at his friends. "What is her official title?"

Caleb felt some of the tension seep out of his muscles. Just thinking about Holden's attempts to get Mia to run off to Las Vegas and get married were enough to break through any bad mood. "Soon-to-be fiancée."

Avery smiled at that description. "She's not sure?"

"Oh, she plans to marry him. She just wants some closure on the case we're working on first. She claims a wedding is inappropriate right now," Caleb explained.

Adam headed for the kitchen. "Drives Holden nuts, which is downright enjoyable to watch."

They all followed Adam's lead. As Luke poured coffee, they took seats around the conference table. Caleb hated the delay. He was two seconds away from gnawing off his arm. He'd had a rough evening and had been more than patient in waiting to hear Avery's story.

Luke must have sensed Caleb's frustration because after one glance in his direction, Luke started the conversation moving. "You showed up at Caleb's condo tonight. Why?"

She closed her eyes as she took a long swallow. "Rod."

Luke's cup stopped halfway to his mouth. "Excuse me?"

Caleb wanted to fast-forward through this part. "Yeah, she knows. Seems to know all about us and what we do."

Luke shook his head. "Not possible."

Avery sighed. "That must be the party line because you've all said it to me now."

"How?" Gone was the calm questioning. Luke had flipped right to angry.

"From Rod," she said.

Caleb took over when Luke just sat there with an openmouthed stare. "Do you know where Rod is?"

"I was hoping you did."

Luke took a deep breath then tipped back in his chair, lifting the front legs right off the ground. "You know we have about four hundred questions about you and Rod and what happened this evening. You up to filling us in?"

"We should let her rest," Adam said as he leaned against the sink.

Caleb felt his patience expire. "We've waited long enough. She can talk now."

When Adam started to argue, she held up a hand to stop him. "It's okay. Caleb is right. Rod contacted me about doing some private, off-the-books DNA testing for him."

"Why you?" Luke asked.

"Let her finish." Caleb didn't like Luke's rushed tone. Understood it but didn't want Avery subjected to more yelling and intimidation.

No matter what their history and how she had treated him, she'd shown a lot of courage tonight. She didn't curl in a ball and cry. She wasn't weak. She did everything he told her to do when he said it and helped them all out of a difficult situation. Sure, she was the reason they were in it, but Rod had placed her in the spotlight.

Caleb once trusted Rod more than he trusted anyone. Now Caleb didn't know what to believe. He grew up with a father who spent more time on overseas deployments than at home, so he understood responsibility and putting the cause first. He had lived his life knowing the greater good sometimes prevailed over a family's needs.

None of that explained Rod's sudden departure. He had the Recovery agents on his side. He didn't need to go off on his own. He could trust the agents with anything and they would support him. It ate at Caleb to think Rod couldn't see that simple fact and made a conscious choice to put Avery, an untrained innocent, in danger instead.

But that wasn't the only thing eating away at Caleb's gut. The intersection of his lives, past and present, of people he didn't even know had met each other, shook him, and not much broke through his outer shell that way.

Avery toyed with the edge of her bag. Ran her fingers

over the seam and concentrated all her energy on the process. "Rod was convinced someone was switching DNA results."

"Of what?" Adam stared at the ceiling for a second. "Or should I say who?"

Her shoulders raised then slumped as she took in a huge breath. "Participants in witness protection."

Luke shook his head. "I don't understand."

"Rod believed women who were supposed to be alive and living under new identities had actually been killed. He said someone knows the yearly check-in schedules and is making plans to cover the murders."

"Damn." Luke said it, but Caleb felt the shock just as strong.

Avery continued. "The theory was that people from their old lives were paying to have them killed."

The magnitude of the corruption hit Caleb like a roundhouse kick to the jaw. His breath rushed out with a string of profanity. "You're talking about a huge conspiracy. Someone in WitSec would have to be in on that. The arrangements between the insiders and the people paying for the hits and the actual killers would be huge."

Luke's face turned red. "And expensive. That's the point, right? Someone on the inside, probably several people, is making big money off this sort of access."

Avery bit her lip. "Unfortunately, yes."

"What did they hope to gain?" Caleb asked.

She stopped fidgeting in her seat and playing with the bag and dropped her arms to the table. Balancing her weight on her elbows, she surrounded her mug with her palms. "I have no idea. Probably revenge or maybe eliminate a trial witness if a case was appealed or required a new trial."

"Glenna Reynolds and Peggy Wain." Caleb felt the pieces click together. They'd found files on Rod's computer about the women. The only information they had was about their participation in witness protection, and even that had been tough to track down due to the program's secrecy. It all made sense now. Rod thought these women were victims.

Avery knocked her fist against the table. "How do you know about them?"

Caleb didn't miss the shock in her tone. "What?"

She rummaged through her bag and took out a fistful of papers. She slammed one against the table. Pointing to the top of a printout she showed them the names Caleb just mentioned. "Those are two of the names of the women I was investigating. Rod believed the bodies he found in a crudely dug grave belonged to them."

"Did they?"

"Yes, but I could only prove those two. I was working on the third when I tried to track down Rod, failed and went looking for Caleb."

"Track Rod down how?" Luke asked.

She smacked her lips together, clearly upset at being interrupted. "We met every Thursday morning. When he stopped showing up at the diner, I double-timed my research, figuring there was a problem. Also started searching for him in the places I knew he frequented. When I went to his condo—"

"You know where he lives?" The shock was evident

in Adam's voice. He seemed more stunned by that bit of news than her meeting regularly with Rod.

"He wasn't there." She waved her hand as if to put this part of the conversation behind her. "The point is no matter what the WitSec records say, these women are dead. Rod was looking for evidence that someone had stepped in and was living their fake lives, or had set up a system to make it look as if the women were still alive."

Caleb almost smiled when he looked at the matching wide-eyed, hollow-cheeked expressions of Adam and Luke. They rarely got flustered, but now looked ready to blow. Caleb decided it was better to stay on track. "You referenced two, Avery. Were there other women? Any men?"

"Rod suspected three women had been eliminated already." She swallowed hard enough for Caleb to see it. "That's his word, not mine."

"And?"

"I hadn't finished my work on the third. I'll need to get to my lab and check."

Anger swamped Caleb, heated his skin from the inside out. Not at Avery but at the idea that someone who swore an oath to protect would abuse that power. He didn't like the idea of Avery walking back into danger either. "Never going to happen."

"I agree with Caleb," Adam said, rushing in before Avery could respond. "Your lab is the first place people will look for you. By now, someone has gone through your computer and paperwork looking for you and knows what you've been working on."

She turned her smile on all of them. "Well, of course. I figured that was a possibility and hid the results."

Caleb had to admire her intelligence and spunk. She could have turned over the evidence she had and then stepped away. Instead, she kept fighting. It was a pretty sexy trait in a woman, even in one who once turned his life upside down.

"Where do you have them?" he asked.

"Oh, they're in the lab and on the system, but under names tied to a fictitious case. My assistant is handling it. He has no idea that he's doing undercover work for Rod." Her mouth flattened. "Wait, is Damon in trouble?"

"Damon is?" Caleb asked.

"My assistant."

The men looked at each other. Caleb spoke up, though he dreaded to see her face when he gave the answer. "He could be."

She stood up, scraping the chair on the cement floor behind her. "We have to go."

Caleb reached out and folded his hand over hers before she could run for the door. The goal was to get her to stop moving, but he hoped to offer some comfort, as well. "We will. I promise. But we have to be smart and ready."

Luke nodded. "Exactly. We'll figure out a plan today. Depending on how much trouble Adam has with the security system, we might be able to go in tonight."

"We only know of two names. What's the third?" Adam asked.

"Maddie Timmons." Avery slipped her hand out from under Caleb's and reached for another paper in her bag.

"If this Maddie person isn't dead, she's in grave danger. Rod wanted to know the answer so he could get word to her. He planned to send Caleb for her."

Luke scanned the documents Avery had provided and dropped them on the table. "One thing I don't get."

"Only one?" Adam asked.

Luke talked right over Adam's mumbling. "How do you know Rod?"

She sat down hard on the chair. "I guess it's too much to ask that we skip that question."

The harsh lines around Luke's mouth eased. "I understand you feel loyalty to Rod, but—"

"It's not that."

Caleb didn't like the change in her. She went from fiery and ready to do battle, to quiet. Rubbing her forehead and evading eye contact wasn't her usual style. He didn't like her subdued and upset.

"What is it?" he asked.

After another minute, she leaned back and crossed her arms in front of her. "Rod was friends with my brother."

Caleb closed his eyes and pushed out all the dark thoughts that ran through his mind before he could focus again. "We don't talk about Rod in the past tense."

"That's not what I meant."

Caleb tried to remember exactly what she said so he could figure out her comment, but he couldn't call it back up. "Tell us."

"I was referring to Ryan in the past. My brother." She pressed her lips together and sat there for a few seconds. "He died in Afghanistan."

"Damn, Avery." Caleb wanted to reach out, to ease the pain he saw straining across her face. "I had no idea."

"I know." She whispered the comment but didn't look at him. Didn't look at any of them. Her glassy stare stayed focused on the table.

Last Caleb knew, Ryan had twenty days left on his deployment. He was in his mid-twenties, young and smart, and the idea of him dying and Avery grieving made Caleb frantic. He wanted to get up and pace, swear and then punch his fist through the wall.

Instead, he tried to keep the shaking rage he felt inside out of his voice. "When?"

"Three weeks after you left—" she took a quick look in Luke's direction "—the job."

This time Caleb took both of her hands in his. With his head low and his mouth close to her ear, he did the only thing he could do. "I'm sorry."

"I know."

He rubbed his thumb over her cheek, waiting to catch any tears that might fall. He knew Avery and Ryan had only each other. Their father raised them until he died of a heart attack while Avery was in college.

Caleb was so lost in her anguish that he didn't hear the warning alarm before the door to the room rolled back on its tracks.

Zach filled the opening, still holding his motorcycle helmet in his hands. "What did I miss?"

Avery's head flew up. She hiccuped back her unshed tears. "Zach?"

He stopped dead. "Avery?"

Caleb felt his life spin out of control even faster. "You two know each other?"

She jumped out of her chair and rushed to Zach. "Good to see you."

The hug lasted all of a second, but that was enough as far as Caleb was concerned. Zach wasn't the type to display a lot of emotion. Definitely not a touchy guy. The half-hearted arm around Avery's shoulder was more than Caleb had seen Zach give anyone.

"How do you know Zach?" Caleb asked, his voice louder this time.

She had the nerve to look confused. "What?"

Caleb stood up and stared Avery down. "I'm trying to figure out how my ex-girlfriend knows all of my friends when I've never introduced you or heard you talk about each other."

If Zach sensed the rising tension, he didn't show it. He shrugged. "I served with Avery's brother."

"We've known each other for years. From before I ever knew you." She gave the explanation in a rushed, no-breathing sentence.

"Did you say ex-girlfriend?" Luke separated each word of the question.

Caleb had had enough of tiptoeing around this part. Everyone had questions but they didn't even understand the bigger issues, like why every aspect of his life was intersecting at one very attractive, very irritating point.

"It all happened before I started here. We were dating, she got a promotion and then fired my a—"

Her hands went to her hips. "That's not how I remember it."

Luke balanced his fists against the table as he rose to his feet. "Wait a second."

When even Zach was staring at her, Avery's hands started moving. One of the nervous gestures almost smacked Zach in the stomach. "None of this matters."

"It's a hell of a coincidence." Luke's voice increased to a near-shout.

Caleb understood Luke's frustration. It bubbled inside both of them. Ties like that raised a red flag. Her connections with his life, all parts of his life, suggested a conspiracy of some sort. She knew about his past and now showed up in his present. It was all so convenient.

Then there was the personal stuff. Luke and Caleb had shared stories. They all knew how Claire once picked another man over Luke. Mutual female betrayal provided an odd sort of bonding and eased Caleb's transition from pure scientist to Recovery Project undercover agent.

Luke got it. Hell, all the men did. None of them liked the idea of being used.

Caleb realized during those long hours over beers he rarely, if ever used Claire's name. At that point in his life he fell back on less flattering references to her. Not his finest moment, but back then he couldn't say it without having his temper flare out of control.

"Zach," Caleb said. "Talk."

"I know Avery through Ryan. We were together in Afghanistan. Holden was there, too." Zach frowned at

Avery. "You're the woman who picked a promotion over Caleb a few years back?"

"Is that what he told you?"

Zach nodded nice and slow. "Yeah."

"It's not true." She sounded furious when she denied it. Worse, she sounded sincere.

Caleb had no idea why she'd pretend. "Are you kidding with this?"

"What?"

"Don't lie."

"I'm not."

Adam pushed away from the sink and stepped between Caleb and Avery. "There's probably a better time to talk about personal stuff. We need to stay focused on the WitSec issues and Rod's suspicions. I want to get the surveillance video from the condo and run face recognition. We'll see if we can identify our attackers."

Relief showed on every inch of Avery's face. "And I'm ready to drop. I could use a few minutes to sit before we do anything else."

Caleb was surprised she didn't hug Adam to thank him for giving her an out. Caleb wanted to punch him. "You look fine to me."

Silence hung in the room until Luke spoke up with a roughness usually reserved for the people they hunted. "Adam's right. Avery can rest upstairs. We have other work to do anyway. Once we fill Holden and Zach in, we have to come up with a plan."

"For what?" Zach asked.

"Someone needs to stick with Avery and get to her assistant to confirm Timmons is alive," Luke said. "If the lady is still with us, we have to track her down and get protection out to her."

Adam nodded. "I can go with Avery."

"She stays with me." Caleb had no idea why he thought it or even when the idea popped into his head. He just knew he wasn't about to leave Avery alone with Adam.

And they had a lot of talking to do. Caleb knew the only way to get her to explain was to give her no other option. That's what he intended to do.

"Do I get a say in who goes with me?" Avery asked.

As far as Caleb was concerned she didn't. "No."

"Why?"

"Apparently we have some history to discuss."

Chapter Six

"We have a problem." Russell delivered his assessment while pacing in front of Trevor's desk.

"Not that I'm aware of." Trevor seriously considered calling security. Making Russell disappear completely held even more appeal. No way would anyone miss this self-important blowhard.

When Russell called and insisted Trevor be available for a meeting for the second time in less than twelve hours, Trevor was tempted to refuse. He'd already wasted his early morning. He refused to lose his evening as well.

"Don't be so sure."

Trevor had reached the end of his patience with this nonsense. "I have work to do that has nothing to do with you or WitSec."

Russell stopped and shot Trevor a smirk of superiority. "You seem to forget how this works."

"Really?" Trevor set his pen down and leaned back in his chair. "Enlighten me."

"You're the one who started this. You came to me for help."

"No, I didn't."

"You had all sorts of questions about divorce law and my past career as a private attorney in that area. And then you mentioned your nasty divorce and your son."

Trevor fought to keep his face blank. He had miscalculated badly and had been paying for that one mistake for more than eight months. When his wife screamed for a divorce, he was taken off guard. There hadn't been any love there for years, but she had free run of his wallet and he was sure that bought him a silent understanding. That illusion exploded when she started making threats about sole custody.

The pushing and badmouthing of him in front of their son snowballed until Trevor asked the wrong person the wrong question about how to get rid of an unwanted wife. It was a momentary lapse, but Russell had a tape of the conversation and kept waving it around. How he got it wasn't clear, since Trevor always prepared for those sorts of things.

What Trevor did know was the tape started Russell digging. When he did, he figured out Bram was using his office to benefit the man accused of trying to kill Claire Samson Hathaway. The blackmail started right after. Russell went after both Walters brothers. He had connections and enough intelligence to cover his tracks. He made contingencies and hid his blackmail evidence to ensure he didn't just disappear.

Money was the motivation. But having Bram check into WitSec files attracted the attention of people in the Recovery Project and led to his death. Trevor had been fighting them ever since.

He cleared his throat. It was either that or launch across his desk and strangle the idiot on the other side. "Everyone knows about my divorce. My wife has seen fit to drag every last detail through the press."

The smirk grew more irritating. "Not all of the details. There are some very interesting facts your wife doesn't know. Imagine what she could do in a custody trial with those."

Trevor vowed to double his efforts to track down the location of those tapes. "What do you want?"

"The Recovery Project."

Russell could get in line on that one, as far as Trevor was concerned. Bram had been gunning for the Recovery agents when he died in a shoot-out in the woods of Virginia. Trevor should have hated them, but he felt only a reluctant admiration for the way they operated.

And then there was the deal. After the last gun battle, he agreed with Luke Hathaway that each would pretend the other didn't exist. It was the only option to prevent mutually assured destruction. Of course, that didn't mean Trevor didn't keep a watchful eye on the Recovery agents. The government believed they had disbanded. Trevor knew better.

He picked up his pen and flipped it end over end, tapping it against his blotter at every turn. "That subject bores me. My brother was obsessed with the group. Let it go. It's been dissolved."

Russell leaned down on the edge of the desk. "Rod Lehman was looking into WitSec. Your brother was digging around."

"With your help. You're the one who wanted information on specific participants. Information you were too low on the food chain at WitSec to obtain." Trevor had to hide his smile when Russell's face turned bright red.

"Since then I've been promoted."

"We're all thrilled. I, for one, sleep better at night knowing you're in charge of something."

"Don't test me, Trevor. You know what I want."

He did not let up with the tapping, not once he caught Russell glancing at the pen and wincing at the noise. "What would that be?"

"Bram broke up the Recovery Project, but that's not good enough. I need Rod found and all of the agents stopped. You can make that happen however you wish, but it has to be permanent and fast."

"Because you're afraid someone will stumble onto your moneymaking scheme?"

Russell shoved away from the desk. "You should be worried as well."

"And why is that?"

"Do you honestly believe I would be dumb enough to let the trail lead back to me? Your fingerprints are all over the files. If someone goes digging, they will see you looking where you shouldn't be looking and how you engaged your dead brother to help you."

"I think you honestly believe you could pull this off." Which showed how truly delusional Russell had become.

Trevor tried to imagine how easy it would be for his people to break into the computer system at the Marshal Service and erase those fake footsteps Russell had planted. And that's exactly what would happen by noon tomorrow. Trevor would go the extra step to make sure all that carefully designed plotting would point directly at Russell as the greedy mastermind and sole participant.

Trevor's company, Orion, ran complex operations all over the world. He had access to whatever he needed in terms of people and resources. The idea that one lower-ranking government worker thought he could take him on and win almost made Trevor laugh.

The only thing he feared was the tape. He had tried to track it down, quietly having his most trusted operatives search Russell's office and home, but Trevor hadn't located it yet. The minute he did, Russell was a dead man.

"I can easily sell the story of you as the instigator. Your company and its, shall we say, specialty area make it very possible you would have the power to go looking where you shouldn't," Russell said.

Looked as if the man had selective memory. When he wanted to prove Orion's power, he praised its abilities. When he wanted to show he was in charge, he pretended he was stronger, more resourceful than Orion.

Trevor wondered, not for the first time, why he didn't just crush this man and risk the consequences. "Interesting."

"Isn't it?"

"So, what is your plan here, Russell?"

"As I said before, end Recovery's interference."

Trevor had heard the same requests from Russell since the day after Bram's funeral. Trevor wasn't any more inclined to help today than he was then. "That sounds suspiciously like you want me to do your dirty work."

"Make it happen now."

"What's the hurry?"

Russell ignored the question. "I would hate for someone in the press to hear a certain tape I have in my possession. Anything happens to me and the tape goes public. If nothing happens to stop Recovery, the price to you is the same. Public exposure, loss of any chance of ever seeing your son again and probably jail time."

"You have it all figured out."

"I do."

Russell didn't have any idea of the wrath he was unleashing against him with these threats. Trevor knew that ignorance would be the man's downfall. "You think you own me."

"I do."

"Let me ask you this." He tapped faster and louder. "Are you done?"

Russell's gaze went to the pen and then back to Trevor's face. "With what?"

"Did you collect the money for the killings?"

Russell froze. He looked at every corner of the room as if just realizing Trevor could be taping him, which, of course, he was.

"Problem?" Trevor asked.

"I got money for information, much like what you do."

"I suppose you sleep fine at night."

After another glance around the room, Russell spoke

louder. "I'm not the one who tried to make my wife disappear."

"But you are the one sitting there, threatening to destroy me no matter what it takes."

This time Russell leaned in. His voice dropped to a whisper as hate filled his eyes. "I'm betting your reputation is more important to you than anything else. After all, isn't that why you covered up the truth about your brother's death?"

Trevor fought off a flinch. Seemed the annoying man had some good instincts after all. "I don't know what you're talking about."

"I'm willing to bet if I dug a little I'd find out his death wasn't so heroic after all."

Trevor carefully laid the pen down on the desk blotter before folding his hands together. "Congratulations."

"So, I'm right."

"I didn't say that."

"Then for what?"

"You are now my number one priority."

Russell's lips curled into a satisfied grin. "I see we finally understand each other."

It was quite clear to Trevor that Russell didn't understand a thing.

AVERY AND CALEB STOOD a hundred feet away from the entrance to her lab. They hovered inside the high-security gate surrounding the property thanks to Adam's ability to unlock it from the safety of the Recovery warehouse miles away.

It was after ten o'clock, and the building was mostly

dark except for the hallway lights that always stayed on. As predicted and right on schedule, the cleaning crew took off an hour earlier. That left a few security guards, and Avery was confident they could dodge them.

"It's time to move." Caleb made the comment from over her left shoulder. Anger still rang in Caleb's voice and radiated off his stiff body.

At least he'd finally stopped arguing. He had spent half the afternoon insisting she stay at the warehouse and let the agents handle the…what did he call it? Information recovery. He reasoned that he knew his way around the labs and building offices since he once worked there, but she refused to give in.

She agreed to help Rod all those months ago knowing the assignment was both a violation of her work contract and a potential danger. She accepted responsibility for her decision and wasn't about to let Caleb walk into a situation she should handle on her own.

"After we do this, is your plan to bury my body somewhere that no one can find it?" She joked but he didn't laugh.

"Nothing so dramatic."

"What then?"

"You heard Luke. We're going to go in there and grab the information and get out. It's that simple, and I haven't thought past that point."

She had heard Luke issue his orders earlier and then leave the building. Getting home to his wife was the excuse he used, but Avery sensed the poor man was sick of fighting with Caleb. She certainly was. Being concerned was one thing. Shutting down and trying to push her out was another.

She didn't have to guess the problem. Caleb was a smart man. The pieces had started falling together in his mind. She knew the people he knew. There was an easy explanation, but he would never believe her. The question was whether he would come out and ask or if she would have to volunteer the information. Probably the latter.

"Are you really going to pretend your foul mood stems from worries about getting into the building?" she asked.

Air blew across her cheek from his sharp exhale. "I'm concentrating on the task ahead of me. Nothing more and nothing less. This is about work."

"Could have fooled me."

He stepped around in front of her. He loomed over her with his arms folded across his broad chest and a fierce scowl plastered on his mouth. "Excuse me?"

As if he scared her. She'd seen him angry before. Furious, even. He could puff up his body until he overwhelmed her, making her feel small and vulnerable. But he wasn't a man who would ever hurt a woman. Not physically.

"At least be honest about it, Caleb. You're angry."

"Way past that, Avery. I'm not denying it."

"Let me guess, once again you're convinced I've gone behind your back and done something terrible. That I've somehow betrayed you." He was big on the betrayal accusation. He'd thrown that word around before he walked out of the office, her apartment and her life.

Two years. He'd turned his back on her and moved on. During all that time she doubted he thought about her even once. Nothing in his welcome when he found her in his condo suggested anything other than distaste. He'd made it clear he never needed her. Now he had his gadgets and his undercover work. Whatever void her absence may have left filled right up with his life inside the Recovery Project.

It had taken her longer to rebound. She guessed that was always the case with the party who got dumped. Back then she wallowed and tried to make him listen. When she couldn't reach him, she went to Rod and tried to save him. Caleb was not a man who could stay idle and unemployed. He was also not the right guy for the strict regulations of a lab. He didn't just run tests. He'd spent time trying to solve crimes, even though that wasn't his job and she begged him to stop. Finally she had no choice but to let him go.

He opened his mouth to say something then shook his head. "Let's drop this discussion."

"Is that your answer for everything? Run away and pretend it doesn't exist?"

"Fine. You want to know the truth?" His jaw clenched as he slapped his hands against his outer thighs. "I don't have a clue what's going on. You walk out of my life two years ago—"

"You kicked me out!"

"Now I find out that you have your hands in every aspect of my life. That you always have." He started counting off on his fingers. "You know my friends and my boss. You have knowledge about Recovery, a group that you shouldn't even know exists. You have a key to my house. And to top it all off, you waltz back into my life just when…"

Her heartbeat hammered in her ears. "What?"

"Nothing." He turned away from her. Stared at the building as if it was the most important thing in the world.

"Do you actually think I'm stalking you?"

When he looked at her again, the anger was back under control. "You tell me."

"I've just been living my life the last two years." Without you, she added silently. "In the beginning I called repeatedly and you refused to answer or respond. You shut me down. I went to your apartment and you told me to leave."

"Do you blame me?"

"Yes."

He didn't roll his eyes, but he sure looked as if he wanted to. "So, when all of this didn't work, you decided to weasel your way into my private life. This way."

The man was completely clueless. Sure, she worked behind the scenes to help him. She told Rod she didn't want anything traced back to her. But a small part of her did. She wanted Caleb to figure it out and come back… begging.

"Yeah, Caleb. I've spent two years setting up this intricate plan to get to know everyone you hang out with. Your mailman and auto mechanic are next." She snorted. "Be serious."

"What am I supposed to think?"

"That I helped you."

"When?"

"Back then."

"By firing me?"

"By finding you the job you wanted." All of the frustration and hurt festered until it blew. She practically screamed the truth in his face.

He pulled back, put a good three feet between them and then shot her one of those you've-lost-your-mind looks he did so well. "What is that supposed to mean?"

"I got you into Recovery. I used my brother's name and his connections with Rod and got you noticed."

"That's not true."

So many bad moments had passed between them that Caleb couldn't even see the truth when it slapped him in the face. The realization sucked the life right out of her. "It is. So, while you're determined to paint me as the bad guy in this situation, and from the appalled look on your friends' faces when they figured out who I was, it's clear that's exactly what you did, you might want to remember that I helped to make this life possible for you."

He shook his head and didn't stop. "You're insane."

"No, Caleb, I'm just tired of standing here talking to you." She pushed past him and headed toward the building's entrance.

"Where are you going?"

"In there. You can come with me or sit out here. I just don't care anymore."

Chapter Seven

Avery kept her head down and her legs moving. She didn't stop until she was right outside the door to the building. Caleb jogged the few steps to catch up with her.

She wouldn't look at him, so he slipped his hand under her elbow and turned her to face him.

Standing there and hearing her take credit for his job with the Recovery Project had made him furious. It took all of his control not to walk right back out of the parking lot and as far away from her as possible. But something in her tone, in the pleading look in her eyes, got to him. It didn't matter if he believed her, and he didn't. She believed it.

He didn't understand why her life continued to intersect with his. He couldn't fit it together with what he remembered and have it make sense. But Zach and Holden—Caleb couldn't deny her connection to them. He searched his brain to call up his first meeting with Rod. Something drew them together. Caleb was not obsessed with finding out what.

"Avery—"

She shrugged his hand off her arm. "My priority right now is to figure out if Maddie Timmons is alive. That should be your goal, too. As you pointed out earlier, nothing else matters. Let's get back to that way of thinking, shall we?"

No one had ever had the audacity to suggest he wasn't committed to a job. To tell him to keep his mind on the job. Yet that was exactly what Avery was doing. She laid out what should be his priorities and dared him to argue.

He forgot until right that minute how infuriating it was to fight with her. Her instincts were to come out swinging. The never-say-die attitude appealed to him. There was something sexy about a woman who fought for what she wanted and needed. Except when you're on the wrong side of all that determination. It's why he had to leave town for two weeks after they stopped dating. When it became clear she didn't plan to ease up, he checked out. It was either that or unload, and he didn't want to give her the satisfaction.

Not then and not know. "Fair enough."

"What, no arguments?" she asked.

"I can admit when you're right."

"Since when?"

"Now who is losing focus?"

Adam coughed in their earpieces. "You both are driving me nuts. Does that help settle this argument?"

Avery covered her mouth and stared at Caleb with wide eyes. "I forgot."

"That happens all the time. I stay quiet and people

forget I'm here," Adam said. "You'd be amazed the garbage I hear."

Caleb muttered a curse. The tiny transmitters on their shirts and microphones in their ears had recorded every nasty word. Every private comment. Adam had overheard it all. He hadn't even bothered to breathe loud and remind them he could hear.

"Thanks for the heads-up," Caleb muttered. He'd do more than that when he got his hands on Adam later. Since the shock on Avery's face was slowly turning to jaw-clenching anger, he guessed she would take a shot at Adam, too.

"This is entertaining and all, but we have a job to do," Adam said as he verbally rubbed the raw spot even more.

"I could say 'she started it' but I'll refrain."

She turned her scowl on Caleb. "Good idea."

He shrugged. "Back to work."

"About time," Adam said.

"You would be wise to be quiet right now," Avery said. "Both of you."

Caleb decided it was well past time to start acting like an agent and do the job he was trained to do. "Are we ready to go in?"

"I've set a delay." Adam's voice switched from amused to businesslike. "Impressive system, by the way. Took me most of the day to work around and get through the security protocols."

"Not a surprise since my lab's work is at the heart of many criminal cases. It wouldn't be good for the prosecution if the results weren't trustworthy and reliable."

"We can congratulate the lab's tech team later," Caleb said. "Tell us what we're supposed to do."

"When Avery swipes her badge, it won't register for eight minutes."

Avery glanced at Caleb before turning her attention back to his watch. "Why eight?"

"It's all I could manage, and that's only because of how I directed the signal internally. It's going to bounce around and give us time. But not much."

"I'd say," Caleb grumbled.

"In fact, make it seven just to be safe."

Avery shook her head. "I have no idea how you do what you do."

"That's what makes me relevant." Caleb could hear the smile in Adam's voice as he said it. "Bottom line is you now have seven minutes to get in, get the information and get out. I can't hold off the imprint longer than that. As it is, anyone checking the system later will see you went in and out when you were supposed to be on vacation unless I can figure out how to erase it without erasing you as an employee."

"How will you explain being here tonight?" Caleb knew she was a stickler for the rules.

"I have no idea."

"From what I can see on the monitors, the guards are one floor up and out of your way. When you're done, go to Zach. He's waiting for you by the delivery entrance. I'll keep him updated on your position and the time frame. He's your ticket out of there," Adam said.

Caleb got the point. "In other words, we need to move it."

"Right. No arguing, just go and everything will be fine."

"Because these things always go according to plan." Caleb could think of thirty things that could go wrong before they even got inside.

Avery sighed. "Humor me and tell me that's true."

He adopted his most serious tone. "Always."

Adam chuckled. "Let me know the second before you swipe and we're good."

Avery held her badge next to the scanner. With one last glance at Caleb, she moved it closer. "Ready?"

He nodded and then gave Adam the signal. "We're going in."

"I'm going radio silent unless there's an emergency. Go ahead and swipe."

With a snap, the double doors opened. A quick walk through the lobby took them to another security check and more doors. Walking through those was like walking back in time. Familiar smells flooded Caleb's senses—the chemicals, the cleaning supplies and the metallic scent given off by some of the equipment. It all came rushing back to him.

His specialty within Recovery was medical and science. His life here had been different. He left the navy, the only job he'd ever trained to do, and turned to what he hoped would be the solace of steady work without a gun. Just showed that nothing ever went as planned.

"Caleb?" She put a hand on his forearm. "Are you okay?"

"Let's do this." At the snap in his voice, she pulled back and he immediately regretted the tone. But now was not the time for apologies and excuses. "Which way?"

"It's across the hall from our old lab."

They rushed down the corridor with her in the lead. Secure doors lined the hall. She stopped at the last on the left. Her badge got her through as easily this time as the first. Looked as if her company considered her to be on a legitimate vacation, because they hadn't pulled her access. For the second time he wondered if they would later and what she would do without this job that clearly meant more to her than anything else.

She pushed open the set of double doors and led them into a large lab. With its shiny surfaces and wall of cabinets, the place should have been spotless. Had to be in order to pass state inspections without trouble.

It looked as if a bomb had gone off. Papers littered the floor. Glass shattered across countertops. A wall unit had been ripped off the wall and smashed to the floor. Every cabinet was open and nothing remained untouched.

"What happened?" Her voice mirrored the horrified look on her face.

"Sabotage."

"All those criminal cases. Everything is in jeopardy now." She took a pen off the floor and picked up the edge of some paperwork. A ripped evidence envelope lay beneath it.

He mentally calculated the loss and realized she wasn't exaggerating.

"There are chain-of-custody issues now. Cross-contamination problems. Defense attorneys will question all of our testing and rip our conclusions to shreds. None of it will withstand scrutiny." She groaned. "Cases will fall apart."

Every word she said was correct. The concerns she voiced weren't frivolous, but Caleb needed her focused. The magnitude of this disaster was one she'd have to work through another time. She and a team of forensic experts, and even then the results would be devastating.

"What do you need from in here?" he asked.

She plopped down on a stool and wheeled it over to a computer. The screen had a huge hole in it. She flicked the switch a few times, but it wouldn't turn on.

"Try another." He tried to sound calm as he made the suggestion.

When she started tapping on the keyboard, he glanced at his watch. The heat imprints for the security guards showed them one floor up as Adam indicated and working from opposite directions. What worried him was the faint shadow in the room next door. It showed up out of nowhere and wasn't very strong. It was either a false read or someone in trouble.

"Adam?"

"I see it. I'll use the security cameras to do a visual check."

At the sound of Adam's voice in their ears, Avery's head popped up. She frowned but didn't argue when Caleb motioned for her to continue working. Their minutes of freedom were ticking down and now they had an unknown next door and potential hostiles nearby.

"I don't see anything, but the heat signature isn't moving," Adam said.

"Is it possible someone could be sleeping in the office next door?" Caleb asked her.

She didn't stop working. "It's a temperature-controlled room with refrigerator compartments. There's no furniture in there, except maybe a stool."

Adrenaline pumped through Caleb. He could feel it race around every part of his body. "Hurry up."

"I can't." The paleness of her face could be described only as bleak.

"What does that mean?"

"It's not here. Nothing is here. My files are all gone."

The worst-case scenario was coming true. "Adam, can we do something from here to make it easier for you to get in the computer system?"

"I already tried. I could get into the security section because it's hooked in with the electrical and there's a dial-out function in case of an emergency. The case files are coded and encrypted."

Caleb shook his head over Adam's unusual chattiness. "And?"

"Doesn't matter anyway. If Avery's directory is gone, it could be erased from the system entirely. Someone with the knowledge to wipe her out should be smart enough not to leave much of a trail, but I'll check. Meanwhile, get out of there and back to the warehouse."

Sounded like a smart plan to Caleb. "Right."

Avery didn't move from the chair. "We can't."

"Well, you'd better do something because those supposed security guys are headed down the stairs and toward your position."

Caleb caught the anxiety pouring through Adam's voice and the phrasing he used. A check of the blueprint on his watch told him why. "Pretty strategic, don't you think?"

She stood up and grabbed Caleb's arm to see the small monitor. The frown had only deepened when she raised her head again. "What am I missing?"

"These guys move in tandem, taking room by room. It's like they've been trained and are launching a strategic assault."

She nodded. "Against me."

"Or something they think you have." He took one last look around the lab. The extent of the destruction kept the alarm bells ringing in his head. "We need to go."

She increased her grip on his arm when he tried to move. "We have to check next door first."

"No."

"Someone could be hurt."

"We'll call the police as soon as we're safe."

"We can sit here, waste time and argue, or you can just agree with me."

"Avery."

"I'm not backing down on this, Caleb."

He remembered that trait all too well. "Fine. When I later say 'I told you so,' you can explain to Luke how we ended up in a hospital."

Caleb tightened his hold on his weapon. With Adam as his eyes, Caleb normally felt pretty secure in his ability to get out of a rough spot. But he had Avery to worry about. This wasn't about him dodging a bullet. It was about making sure she got into Zach's waiting car in exactly the same condition as she was now. Caleb didn't care what happened to him, but he suddenly cared very much about what happened to her.

They slipped out of the lab and stared down the hallway. He couldn't hear anything except the whirl of the fans above his head and the breathing thundering in his head. He covered her as she opened the door to the room next door. When she slid inside, he followed and closed the door behind them without a sound.

She stopped in the middle of the room and turned around in a circle. Her bewilderment crashed into him. He couldn't blame her. There was nothing in there, just an empty room with some shelves and four steel doors to refrigerator compartments.

"I don't see anyone," she whispered.

He walked over to the area where a body should be. There was a large metal door with the usual security protections. "This is the right corner. Must be inside here."

She slid her card through the reader, but the light didn't turn green.

Caleb couldn't worry about colors. He was busy keeping an eye on his watch and the men he knew were in the building and crowding in closer. They were at the other end of the hall and moving in fast. "We're running out of time."

"This doesn't make sense. The door should open."

"And we should be out of here. One more time then we go."

He watched her rub her badge on his pants and then move closer to the panel. Something crunched under her foot. Keeping his gun aimed at the door, Caleb bent down and grabbed the piece of plastic sticking out from under a metal rolling tray. A badge.

"It's Damon's." Her hands shook as she turned it over.

"Don't borrow trouble. We don't know he's hurt."

"Get out of there," Adam said in a break from protocol. The aberration signaled to Caleb just how much trouble Adam thought they were in.

She ran her hand over the door. "Damon is in here. I can feel it."

The men were just a few doors down now. They weren't talking to each other. Weren't making any noise at all. No security guards Caleb knew moved like this. These two had the skills of a tact team. Synchronized and stealthy. And deadly.

"He must have changed the code to match his card." She straightened out the bent card and then closed her eyes for a second. "Please have that be the case."

When she slid Damon's badge through for the third time, the green light finally switched on. Caleb blocked her from opening the door. He put a finger over his mouth and tried to cover the door to the room, her and whatever loomed in the enclosed space. Danger could fly at them from two angles now.

After motioning for her to squat down in the corner between a shelf and the refrigerator door, he eased it open just an inch. When nothing happened, nothing flew out and the room stayed quiet, he pulled harder and looked inside. There in the five-by-five room, among the glass-front cases filled with vials and boxes, were two bodies. Both motionless and piled in a stack, lying in a pool of blood. He recognized a security uniform on one and a lab coat on the other.

Before he could warn Avery about their find, the glass window next to the room's main door exploded. The staccato thump of bullets hitting against the walls drowned out the sound of her scream. Glass sprayed and the walls shook. Dust kicked up as the ceiling tiles fell. It was a shower of paper and equipment as he grabbed her arm and dragged her inside the enclosed space, tucking her safely behind him.

He felt the thumping impact each time a shot hit the metal door he used as a shield. The steady rain of shots came from the hallway. As fast as it started the echo of gunfire stopped. Aiming his weapon, he vowed to take out anyone who came one foot into their crowded space. With the door open only a sliver, he waited for the men to break into the room and start a second round.

Behind him he could hear Avery shuffling. She talked softly to Damon. Caleb had no idea if the other man was alive. He couldn't worry about that. Not while he waited for commandos to shoot their way inside. There was only one way in and one way out.

"Check." He said the word as soft as possible to let Adam know they were okay.

The hallway lights blinked off, bathing the room in complete darkness. She gasped and grabbed the back of Caleb's shirt.

He could feel her nerves jumping. "Adam?"

"Not me." Adam whispered the comment but Caleb picked it up. These guys were serious and hell-bent on wiping out any witnesses.

"Override and turn them back on in five." Caleb mouthed the words, keeping his tone so low that it was barely audible even to his own ears.

The attackers were on the move. He could sense them as much as hear them. When footsteps crunched, he knew they had breached the outer office and time was almost up. He began the countdown, hoping Adam had heard his whispered plea. The lights flickered just as Caleb got to number one. All around them equipment whirred to life. Both men froze for a split second, which was all the time Caleb needed. He stood up and fired twice, not bothering to wound. No way was he risking they'd be saved by protective vests.

One shot to each forehead and they dropped backward, sprawled and unmoving.

Caleb shoved the door open to survey the damage and check for any sign of life.

Nothing.

He blew out a long breath, trying to drag enough oxygen into his lungs. It took Caleb another second to realize Avery had never let go of his shirt and Adam was screaming in their ears.

"We're okay," Caleb said before Adam brought the walls down trying to find them.

"I can't believe…" Her voice shook as hard as her body. Her fingers trembled, knocking her knuckles against his back.

Reality came roaring back. This was his life, not

hers. She'd held it together, helped him. There was so much he didn't understand about why she showed up and what happened after they broke up, but he admired her rock-hard determination. When everything fell apart around her, she held it together. In that moment, their history didn't matter.

He turned and wrapped an arm around her shoulders and pulled her in close. The immediate warmth of her body next to his relaxed him. He hadn't forgotten the soft scent of flowers in her hair or how good she felt cuddled against him.

Knowing it was stupid, he leaned down and placed a quick kiss on her lips. Once his lips met her soft mouth, the temptation to linger and relearn the taste of her grabbed him, but he pushed it out of his head. This was about providing comfort only. About giving them a moment to celebrate being alive.

The touch was over before it started, but that didn't stop her eyes from growing huge in surprise. "Caleb?"

"What about your assistant?" he asked, dreading the answer.

She shook her head but didn't say anything as she swallowed several times. The sad resignation on her face nearly broke him. His eyes searched hers before wandering lower. The only thing he saw was her kissable mouth.

"Caleb?" Adam's voice didn't sound any steadier than Avery's.

The spell broke. Caleb reluctantly separated their

bodies, letting air pass between them as he tried to push the idea of kissing her out of his head.

Her hands remained wrapped in the front of his shirt. "Caleb, please."

He loosened her grip and set her away from him. "No."

"No?"

He had to get his mind back on the job. Had to make sure that wall he'd erected two years ago stayed solid. If he allowed her to mean something again, he'd regret it.

"Adam? Call Luke. We have two innocents and two attackers down. He's going to have to figure out who to call to clean this up."

Chapter Eight

Avery hadn't thrown up in a decade. She came close to ending that run twice within the last hour. Even now as she sat at the Recovery conference table drinking a soda, she wondered if she should just crawl into the bathroom and sleep there.

Caleb didn't look any better. His hair wore the finger marks from where he'd been running his hand through it. Exhaustion edged around his eyes. During the shoot-out at the lab he'd somehow ripped the front of his shirt, making him look even rougher and more dangerous than usual.

With his elbows on the table, he traced his fingers over the smooth top. He'd been debriefed by Luke since they got back. In a flat tone, Caleb laid out what had happened and how they got through it. The brief flair of adrenaline-fueled attraction from the lab, none of it lingered now. He was no-nonsense to the point of sounding totally uninterested.

"Okay. I think I got it." Luke stretched out in his seat with his hands behind his head. The chair leaned back to the tipping point. "Any chance these were Trevor's men?"

Caleb nodded. "Sure moved like them."

She'd followed every word from a distance, letting Caleb explain while she sat there and fought for control of her stomach muscles. But this part was new. "Who's Trevor?"

The cold indifference disappeared. Caleb actually sneered at the mention of the other man's name. "Trevor Walters, owner of Orion Industries. Multimillionaire, entrepreneur and all-around scumbag."

The name immediately registered, but the description didn't match anything she knew. The guy was a billionaire or close to it. Trevor Walters showed up on news shows and frequently testified on Capitol Hill.

"He's supposed to be a legitimate businessman," she said.

"He had his private militia swarm my house. Had to replace the hardwood floors after that one." Luke's chair landed back on the floor with a thump. "Trust me, calling him a scumbag is a compliment."

Surely information like that would get out. There was no way Trevor Walters could be who they said he was and still function at the level he did…right?

"He seems so, I don't know, stable. I swear I saw him opening an orphanage in some war-torn country."

Caleb shot her a you're-so-naive frown. "He's corrupt, not stupid. He knows when and how to throw his money around to gather favors and prestige, but don't confuse that with chivalry. He won't hesitate to remove anyone who threatens his privileged world."

"Caleb is right. I've dealt with Trevor," Luke said. "We all have."

They were trying so hard to convince her, when that wasn't necessary. "I didn't doubt what you were saying. It's just so hard to imagine."

"He has a significant number of men at his disposal. They're well armed and well trained. Loyal and tough, these are not the kind of guys you can buy off or win to your side with some sweet talk. The good news is we've stopped a bunch of them." Caleb's chest didn't puff up with pride, but it was there in his voice, in the way he sat up straight and didn't flinch when his gaze met hers.

"Meaning you killed a bunch of them."

He didn't hesitate. "Yes."

She didn't judge him. The news actually gave her comfort. Working in a lab, dealing with evidence from horrific criminal cases, she'd developed a practical view of protection. Some people had to be stopped, and from what she could tell the Recovery agents excelled at the task.

The speaker above the door beeped right before the door rolled open. Caleb reached for his weapon and Luke shifted in his seat. They didn't need to worry. The visitor was more than welcome.

Holden came through with a swagger. "Good thing I got here when I did. Sounds like you're giving away all our secrets."

His amusement was contagious. For a second the weight pushing down on her lifted. Or it did until she glanced at Caleb and saw him scowling.

Holden tapped Caleb on the back of the head and then

kept walking until he stood next to her chair. "Avery Walker."

She smiled up at him. "I thought you were going to hide from me forever."

"Never that." Holden winked before pulling her to her feet for a hug. "Zach told me you'd thrown in with us."

"How did Zach come to that conclusion?" Caleb asked.

"He also filled me in on a little secret you've been hiding. The six-foot frowning one right across the table." Holden kept an arm around her shoulders. When Caleb flashed an obscene gesture, Holden just laughed. "Have to wonder what you ever saw in our friend here."

Since her fizzled relationship with Caleb ended on as sour a note as possible, it was just about the last thing she wanted to talk about to a crowd. She skipped the conversation and focused on Holden. "I hear you're an almost-engaged man."

Holden's broad smile faded. "No almost. I *am* engaged."

Caleb laughed. "Does Mia think so?"

After a man-to-man scowl session, Holden returned to his lighthearted mood. "Admittedly, the getting-married part is taking a bit longer than I expected."

"We're all waiting for Mia to come to her senses," Luke said.

Holden guided Avery back into the chair and then plunked down next to her. "Mia wants our lives to be normal first."

From the look of the high-tech room and the number

of times she'd been chased in the past two days, Avery doubted these guys knew what normal was. They thrived on danger and were at home handling guns and breaking into places they weren't supposed to be. The only time they got twitchy, as far as she could tell, was when they were sitting around doing nothing, as they were now.

She had to ask the question just to see if they were aware of how they came off to regular people. "Are your lives ever normal?"

"That's what I'm trying to explain to Mia. It's never going to get better."

The urge to scream *I knew it!* swamped Avery. She had watched Caleb try to fit in to a nine-to-five office existence. He left the navy at his then-wife's insistence. When his marriage broke apart right after, he was already stuck in a career he didn't want, in the same lab with Avery.

She walked into the bitter aftermath only a month after the divorce was final. A smart woman would have stayed clear and let Caleb wallow and complain to his male friends while drowning his frustrations over a few beers. That had been her plan…before he asked her out. Then every intelligent thought went out of her head. The attraction swept through her and took her common sense right along with it.

She never could resist Caleb. From his eyes to his always-mussed hair to those shoulders, everything about him worked for her. Even now, after all that had passed between them, she couldn't hate him. Worse, since their near miss at the lab, she kept staring at his mouth and remembering what he could do with it.

"I'd love to meet Mia, fiancée or not," Avery said.

"Soon but not now." Luke's voice boomed through the room, highlighting every inch of his leadership role.

Holden lazily sprawling in the chair, wasn't all that impressed with the show of temper. "Luke is a bit over-protective at the moment."

"I'm just trying to keep her safe."

Avery assumed the "her" in question was his wife, Claire. Avery knew about Claire's past. Anyone who owned a television knew. Being wrongly accused of her former husband's murder and then being nearly killed by him when he turned out not to be dead made her a bit of a news hero.

These couples—Luke and Claire, Mia and Holden—made Avery smile. For a group of men who moved in shadows and guarded their privacy, they seemed to pick women who dragged them out into the light.

She wondered if Caleb would ever let a woman mean that much. Love required sacrifice and she couldn't see him making that leap. Not again. Not after his first wife had him change everything about his life and then walked out anyway. Even now as he lounged in his chair, he watched her with heat behind his eyes and a lazy interest that spoke more to lust than anything deeper.

Avery broke eye contact with him and turned back to Luke. "Is Claire in danger right now?"

The corner of his mouth tugged up in a small smile. "Not the way you think. She's pregnant."

Holden nodded with a satisfied grin. "That's great news."

"Absolutely. Why didn't you say anything?" Caleb asked.

Luke waited until the rounds of congratulations and backslapping stopped. "We wanted to make sure she was okay. We went to the doctor last week, and she's doing great. She's nine weeks along now and refusing to relax for even a second. She's been back and forth to lawyers setting up the funds we need for Recovery. She's worried about finishing the warehouse and helping Mia and Holden get settled."

"Sounds like the Claire I know."

The softness in Caleb's voice caught Avery's attention. Whenever anyone mentioned Claire, he smiled. He wasn't a man who let women in. A lousy marriage explained part of his reaction. Growing up with a military father and no mother probably explained the rest. He respected his father but rarely saw him. That nurturing aspect just wasn't there, and Avery couldn't break through to give it to the adult Caleb. Heaven knows she'd tried.

But Claire meant something special to him. Avery felt a twinge of jealousy not because she viewed the woman as a rival, but because Claire had won something precious. Something Avery had wanted so desperately from him and never received.

Holden laughed. "And it's killing Claire that she hasn't been over here to get a good look at Avery."

"Why?" she asked.

"She wants to see the woman who…" Luke coughed. Then he did it two more times. "Uh, the woman who got into Caleb's condo and got the jump on him."

"Man, that was a terrible cover," Caleb mumbled.

Avery thought so, too. She understood that they had heard only Caleb's version of their history, and she'd bet her master's degree she didn't come off well in that scenario. They viewed him as the victim and her as the evil troll who wronged him. Rather than be offended, she respected their loyalty to Caleb. Would have been nice if someone could race to her rescue the same way, but no one bothered. Not since Ryan died.

"Anyway, Claire is officially going to be the death of me." Luke dropped his head in exaggerated defeat. "She spent half of last night giving me her theories on Rod and his whereabouts instead of just going to sleep."

"Claire spent the morning throwing up. That's how I figured out she was suffering from morning sickness," Holden said. "Well, Mia figured it out, but I'll take the credit."

Luke sat back in his chair, groaning as he did. "Claire is determined to be a part of this and I am determined to keep her at the house and guarded until this is all over, even if I have to tie her to the bed to do it."

"Isn't that how she got pregnant in the first place?" They all laughed at Caleb's joke.

At least Avery now knew why she'd been separated from the other women. Avery didn't realize it bothered her until the reasonable explanation was in front of her. "And you're staying with Luke to be a bodyguard?"

Holden shrugged. "I'm there because my house blew up. Until my new place is built, Luke's made room for us."

"Mostly for Mia, but Holden seems to come along with the deal," Luke said.

They talked about explosions and getting rid of dead bodies as if those events happened every day. They mentioned them and then moved on. Most people would curl up in a ball on the floor and weep.

"Uh, did you say blew up?" Avery asked.

"You can thank Trevor's brother, the former congressman, for that one," Caleb said.

When she tried to ask a follow-up, Holden shook his head. "It's not worth talking about, and I can't without wanting to dig him up and kill him all over again."

"Speaking of the congressman…" Luke hesitated just long enough to get Holden scowling.

"Here we go," Caleb said.

"David Brennan wants to see us." Luke smiled at Holden. "Not you."

She knew the name because it had been all over the news. David had been handling the office since Bram's death and was viewed as Bram's probable successor. The connections came together in her head and she looked at Caleb for confirmation. "Wait, is Mia the same Mia the congressman saved?"

"No," Holden practically shouted the answer.

Luke winced. "Sort of."

"He died after he tried to kill Mia. The rest is a story made up to appease the press and buy us time while we tried to figure out Bram's connection to the WitSec women." Caleb delivered the abbreviated plot and then stared at her as if willing her to understand.

Avery wasn't sure what she was supposed to get, but

something. A powerful man, someone digging around WitSec. The idea seemed impossible yet… "Oh."

Caleb nodded along with her. "And I can see you understand. I can almost see you thinking."

"There's just no end to the surprises around here." She whispered the thought as the puzzle pieces moved around in her mind.

"I'll fill in the details later. If I do it now, Holden's head will explode," Caleb said.

Holden made a noise somewhere between a growl and a shout. "I'm not ready to talk about Bram Walters or the deal we made with Trevor to cover it up."

There it was. She knew she shouldn't be surprised at the circles they moved in or the wealth of information at their disposal, not after everything else she'd learned. They were undercover, but they did the type of work powerful people needed done. People not on most people's speed dials.

She decided to take the conversation off Mia to ease the tension thumping through the room. Since Holden's grab on the edge of the conference table threatened to break the wood in half, she started there. "David Brennan doesn't like you?"

"I hit him once and he's harboring a bit of a grudge." Holden frowned. "He'll get over it. Eventually."

She looked around the room and sighed. "Is there anyone you guys haven't ticked off or fought with?"

"No." Holden and Caleb gave their views at the same time.

Luke pretended to think about it. "Not really."

So much for trying to make a point. "Do we trust this guy Brennan?"

"Hard to know for sure, but my instincts say yes. He's not Bram and from what I can tell he didn't know anything about his former boss's questionable dealings," Luke said.

Caleb didn't look convinced by Luke's speech. "But he's digging into something or he wouldn't be calling."

"True but I'm not sure what he wants. He just said he had some questions. It could be that simple."

Caleb shook his head. "Never is."

"Since he called himself and didn't have a low-level staff member do it, I'm guessing this is a confidential talk." Luke pointed around the room. "Caleb, Avery and I will head over there tomorrow."

Her heart jumped. "Me?"

"I'm pretty sure this has to do with the WitSec issue. That means you could be our expert if he has a question."

Luke glanced at Holden. "You can watch the women at my house. Zach and Adam will work from here. Adam's still searching through the lab files and trying to get a lead on the Timmons woman. You can check out the list of places where Avery said she'd met with Rod. Maybe we'll get lucky."

She could tell from their silence no one believed that. "What does the chief of staff and possible future congressman want?"

Caleb took that one. "Answers."

IT TOOK A FEW MORE HOURS to send everyone home and clear out the warehouse. Since Avery didn't have anywhere to go and Caleb wasn't about to leave her alone, they were stuck there together.

Now he knew what true torture was.

He had turned off the lights downstairs except for the sensor lights on the outside of the building. Security images flashed on the monitors, showing all angles of each of their private residences and the warehouse grounds. Adam had rigged the system to watch over them yet maintain a measure of privacy. Every minute was recorded and saved for later viewing, if needed.

But Caleb didn't care about any of that right now. His sole focus was on maintaining the control he needed to get back downstairs and leave her alone tonight. The longer he stayed in her presence, the more he wanted her. The more he wanted her, the more he forgot to hold on to his anger.

Sex was the one aspect of their relationship that had always worked. The need burned hot enough to singe. Their first date started with dinner and ended with him not leaving her apartment for two days. He knew the wild, instant attraction had been new for her. For him it was a balm for the sexless marriage he had come to despise and finally put behind him. Avery challenged him outside the bedroom and pleasured him in it.

That was his only excuse for limiting all his interactions with women since their breakup to detached sex with women who didn't matter. Seeing Luke with Claire and Holden with Mia had shifted something inside Caleb. It figured that just when he opened up to the idea of getting involved with a woman again, Avery would waltz back into his life.

For the fiftieth time that evening Caleb wished she had fangs. Anything to kill his desire. He didn't want to want her, tried desperately not to look at her. But everything around him was conspiring to make the wall he built against her crumble.

There was only one light in the corner of the upstairs loft. The way she stood next to it highlighted her tan legs. When she rubbed one bare foot up to her other calf, he thought about tumbling her across the mattress and seeing if she moaned and moved the way he remembered.

As much as he tried to keep the memory of her betrayal in his head, to stoke it and let it fester, it wouldn't stay there. He wanted to conjure up the moment she fired him. Instead, he saw her fighting beside him in the lab and heard her voice shake as she insisted she was responsible for his position in Recovery.

"Who will stay up here once the warehouse is done?" she asked, breaking into his dangerous mental wanderings.

"Whoever needs to. It's a crash pad if we can't get home or need somewhere safe." He made the mistake of looking up and saw nothing but toned legs. Before his brain could send the message to his eyes, his gaze went higher, ending at the edge of her pajama shorts. Mia had Holden bring them over, and Caleb couldn't decide if he should be grateful for the sensual torment or insist Avery wear jeans to bed tomorrow.

"You don't have to go to any trouble for me."

Her husky voice rumbled around in his head. "It isn't much."

"Still."

They hadn't finished the build-out up here. Hadn't even dragged furniture up, so he pulled a mattress across the floor of the loft. "You'll be more comfortable up here. And you deserve a good night's sleep."

"Where will you be while I'm sleeping?"

"On the old couch downstairs." Not that he planned to sleep. Being separated by a five-foot-thick cement floor wasn't enough of a barrier. Not with Avery. He'd likely spend the whole night pacing. Or dunking his head under the faucet in the kitchen.

"It's a love seat and you'll never fit."

"It will be fine."

She walked around the mattress to stand right beside him. If he moved one inch he could rub his cheek against her thigh. If he stood up, he could pull her into his arms and inhale the floral scent that had hovered around her since her shower. But if he just sat there and concentrated on garbage or something equally unsexy, he might have a chance at pushing back the erection pressing against his zipper.

Her fingers trailed along his shoulder. "I have a suggestion."

This couldn't happen. He repeated that phrase over and over. "Uh-huh."

"We can sleep on the same bed."

He stood up fast enough to get dizzy. "Excuse me?"

She closed the small distance between them and rested her hands against his chest. "We're adults."

Fire roared through him, igniting every inch of skin in its wake. "If you say so."

"I'm having very adult thoughts about you right now."

"Huh."

She flashed him smile. "Am I supposed to know what that half grunt means?"

He covered her hands with his. The goal was to stop her from caressing his skin through his shirt. But his good intentions faltered. The feel of her soft skin took his mind in a different direction. The way he figured it, he had two seconds to end this before their clothes hit the floor.

"You know what will happen if we keep going." He meant to drop his arms and step back. Instead, he brushed his thumbs over the back of her hands.

She smiled up at him. "Because you can't control yourself around me."

His breath caught in his throat. "Yeah, exactly. That's right."

"Since when?"

"Don't act surprised." He brought her hand to his mouth and kissed her palm. "You have to feel it. You know there's never been a question about that part of our relationship."

"I know what I want, but I thought you hated me."

He toyed with lying. He could say no and move on to seduction, or he could admit to his confusion. "Me, too."

"I never meant to hurt you." All color leeched out of her face. "I tried—"

Not now. "Don't talk."

"We need—"

"This." Then his mouth was on hers and his hands slipped around her waist.

When her fingers plunged into his hair, his body started to shake. His arm anchored her against him as his lips crossed over hers. The feel of her skin against his, her soft kisses against his chin had him grabbing her backside and drawing her even closer.

Their bodies fit together as he remembered. Their mouths slanted over each other until the sounds of their sharp breathing filled the room. With hands and mouths they welcomed each other again. He couldn't get enough of her, couldn't get close enough.

Couldn't stop.

When she slid down his body to kneel at his feet, he almost lost his mind. They could have this. They had to have this.

Her fingers fumbled with his belt as his palms smoothed through her hair. He hadn't forgotten the silky feel of its length and the indescribable sight of watching her push down his pants and free his erection to her waiting hands.

"Avery."

Then he was in her mouth and he lost the ability to speak or think. All he could do was feel. The press of her mouth on him, the touch of her fingers against his length. She reeled him in and left him dizzy and wanting.

"Be sure, Avery." Inside he begged her to keep going.

In answer, she leaned back against the mattress with her arms thrown out to the side. Her breasts pushed against her shirt every time she dragged in a harsh breath. Those hips lifted off the bed as her legs fell from side to side. She stared up at him with eyes cloudy from desire.

Every ounce of fight fled. Pushing her away seemed inconceivable now.

And she wanted him. That fact screamed through every pore and seared a path into his brain. Two years later, they hadn't lost the spark. She was still the sexiest thing he'd ever seen. He tore off his jeans and underwear and dropped to his knees in front of her. With her legs straddling him, he brushed his fingers up her naked thighs. "I missed this."

"I missed you."

He stripped off her pajama bottoms and the tiny slip of white panties underneath. Then his hands were on her, his fingers in her. A winding groan escaped her lips as he found the spot that made her hips buck and her head press back against the cushion.

When she sat up and peeled his shirt up and off, he lost all control. Forget slow and easy. Forget savoring. He had to be inside her.

Grabbing for his discarded jeans, he tugged the condom out of the back pocket and ripped it open. She helped him roll it on before pressing back into the mattress again. He followed her down and braced his weight on his arms as his mouth dipped down for another long, aching kiss. When he raised his head again, she slipped her hands behind his neck and pulled him back to her.

The kissing and touching took him to the brink faster than he thought possible. One minute he was cupping her breast, feeling the heat seep into his palm, and the next he felt her fingers guide him inside her. With one swift thrust, he pushed long and deep. Panting mixed with moving. Friction caused a tightening in his gut. The in and out of their bodies engulfed them both.

She clasped her thighs against him as her hands glided down his damp back. Her fingernails dug into his skin and her insides pulsed around him. The crash of sensation turned the building inside him into an explosion. He let go and together they rushed headlong into release.

Collapsed on top of her, he could hear the whirl of the fans above him and dull buzz of the machines on the floor below. He lay there and tried to slow his breathing. Worries and doubts assailed him. He had no idea what this meant, if it went beyond simple sex. With all that was happening and everything he knew about Avery slowly shifting in his mind, he couldn't process it all.

A few minutes later, he opened his eyes and realized he was crushing her into the mattress. "You okay?"

"Very."

He placed a string of kisses along her jawline. "I think I passed out there at the end."

Reluctantly, he rolled off her. With his arm thrown over her stomach, he nestled next to her. He'd almost fallen asleep when he heard her sharp intake of breath. He knew she intended to launch into a deep discussion, and he put a stop to it before it ruined everything.

"We've always communicated on this level. Let it be enough right now."

Her hand stilled in his hair. "Is that good enough for you?"

"Yes." For now it had to be.

Chapter Nine

Russell paced the floor in front of his window. At a little after six, the workday hadn't started in earnest. He was the only one in the office, but Beltway traffic and rush-hour commutes dictated that others would start pouring in soon.

By the time the doors officially opened he might have a solution. The loose ends kept stumping him. He had Trevor Walters under control, but he had to finish the Timmons job before the buyer got antsy. Then he had to eliminate Avery Walker. He never expected her to be an issue. The petite woman had wiped out two trained mercenaries.

No, that was wrong. The Recovery Project was behind this latest setback. Their agents' footprints were all over this. They took down attackers, hid the bodies, created a backstory and then launched a behind-the-scenes investigation into their identities and funding. Russell had watched Bram go through this cycle. Even with all his power, the man couldn't derail a couple of unfunded, uncontrolled agents.

Bram had self-destructed. He let a woman in his

office destroy everything. Russell had been rushing around trying to clean up the mess ever since. He had more than a hundred thousand dollars to show for his organizational work. That went a long way to digging him out of the financial hole he was in, but he had hoped for more. With the cover tight, he could have done more jobs, had more business. He was amazed at what people would pay to gain a little revenge, how easy it was to make someone with a false identity disappear.

Not that anyone ever cared about these women. They sucked off the system. They committed crimes and never had to pay for them. An extortionist. The wife of an assassin. Even the one who claimed to be innocent but wasn't. Her file proved her to be a meth dealer.

He'd spent his entire work life listening to program participants whine about how hard it was to leave their old lives behind while they took the money and opportunities provided by honest taxpayers. The world was better without them.

It would be better off without Ms. Walker, too.

The Recovery agents could try to save her, but he was one step ahead of them. He had his men stationed at every location where the Walker woman might turn up. She thought she was so smart, running tests after office hours and burying the results.

She was a loose end. She stood between him and guaranteed freedom.

She had to go.

THE RECEPTIONIST USHERED Caleb, Luke and Avery into the large office formerly occupied by Bram Walters and now used by David in the Rayburn House Office Building at exactly nine o'clock the next morning. Introductions didn't take long since they all knew each other except for David and Avery.

While the three of them squeezed on the blue leather sofa, David sat in a chair on the opposite side of the oriental carpet. From the dark blue suit to the calm demeanor, David looked every bit the politician. Not bad for a guy who worked his way up from answering phones to the chief of staff spot for his predecessor.

Now David was the one in charge, and he took over the conversation. "I'm sure I don't have to tell you how important it is that this information stays between us."

"And my team," Luke corrected.

"Of course."

Caleb still wasn't sure what the information was. He'd never been a fan of showing up on demand, which was part of the reason he attended the Naval Academy. His father believed Caleb needed the structure and discipline. Caleb conceded only because the idea of service appealed to him. Still, letting someone else run the agenda grated. Luke, fine, because the man was born to lead. An outsider, no.

David crossed one leg over the other. "When I started looking through Congressman Walters's private papers following his death, I found some interesting... information."

When he didn't continue, Avery pushed him along. "Yes?"

"I hadn't been privy to this information even though

I ran the congressman's schedule and was in and out of his office every day."

Caleb remembered Holden breaking into Bram Walters's office in an attempt to find that sort of information and finding David instead. Sounded as if David eventually stumbled over it.

Luke leaned forward. "When you say information..."

"It's the sort of documents and background one might keep in a secret compartment in one's desk."

If the man said "one" one more time, Caleb might strangle him. It might be a felony, but it would be worth it. "If you're worried about ruining Bram's reputation with us, don't bother. We know he lied and cheated his way through his term."

"It is possible he bent the rules to fit his purposes," David conceded.

"Talk about an understatement," Luke said.

"I know you have a personal stake in this." David's tone went from welcoming to serious. "If it is something that will cloud your judgment—"

Luke stopped the building tirade. "The man is dead. He can't hurt my wife or Recovery any longer, so as far as I'm concerned that issue is over."

Caleb sat next to Avery and could see her rubbing her hands, feel her fidgeting in her seat. If she wound any tighter, she might blow.

"Why don't we get to it? Why are we here?" he asked.

David unfolded his long legs and went to his desk. When he sat back down in front of them, he handed a folder to Luke. "It would appear Congressman Walters was in possession of confidential documents he should not have had."

"From WitSec," Avery said, cutting through the drama.

"Exactly."

It was Caleb's turn to move around. He shifted until his elbows rested on his knees. Scanning the top of the first sheet in Luke's hands told Caleb what he needed to know. "This is about Maddie Timmons."

"You'll see Russell Ambrose's name in the file. He wasn't Timmons's handler, except for a brief period before his recent promotion. It looks as if Congressman Walters tried to contact Russell. I have no idea if that was successful. When I inquired I received the expected response that WitSec members were not under my purview. John Tate at Justice tried to help but couldn't provide any information I didn't already have."

"So the people in charge know you're investigating the program?" Avery tensed as she asked the question.

David frowned. "Not investigating. Inquiring. And their reactions were appropriate. I don't debate that. It's just difficult to look into the matter quietly and without implicating my former boss, if I can't figure out what that folder is or why he had it."

Caleb could feel her body turn to stone beside him. He understood why even if David didn't. Caleb bit back a groan of frustration. "When did you make the inquiries?"

David's eyebrow lifted. "Last week. Why?"

Caleb glanced at Avery and saw the bleakness he felt

mirrored in her eyes. "If we're right, someone in WitSec is selling access to program participants. Your boss was in this mess up to his expensive haircut."

A flash of fury showed in David's face, but he quickly wrestled his expression back under control. His voice, however, did not hide his shock. "Unbelievable."

Caleb didn't detail the worst of it. David's horrified expression said he understood the magnitude of what he was hearing. If he knew the stolen WitSec information was then used to cash in on murders, he might demand an investigation that could ruin everything. "It's nasty business and Walters wasn't working alone. He needed someone on the inside."

David was a smart man. It didn't take long for him to put it all together and realize they had a problem. "And you're afraid I've tipped that person off."

"It's likely the information has been flagged, looking for activity," Luke said. "Your questions probably got people checking, which means the parties involved in the corruption and cover-up likely have a head start in covering their tracks."

Caleb appreciated Luke's diplomacy but thought David needed a splash of truth. "If she's not already dead, she could be soon. That's the end result we're talking about here."

"How will we know?" Avery voiced one of Caleb's many concerns.

Looking at her now he saw fatigue in the slump of her shoulders and worry around her eyes, but something else lingered there. Hope. In that minute he knew she was as determined as he was to save Maddie Timmons and find Rod. She may have started this process as a favor to Rod, but she was involved now. This wasn't about handing the case off as she did in her regular job. This was about digging in and being involved.

For the first time, Caleb thought she got it. She could see what held him, what made him go beyond his previous lab career. Seeking truth was an addiction.

David frowned. "Excuse me? I don't understand the question."

"The people who set up this plan also set up decoys and dummy files. We don't have photos or know what the real Maddie looks like. That means we don't know if the woman in that house is actually her or not. We're at a huge disadvantage here," Avery explained.

"Thanks to David we now have an address and an old name. Adam should be able to track down her previous life and find a photo." Luke's voice stayed calm.

Caleb knew the relaxed facade was more than that— fake. They'd worked together long enough for him to recognize the seconds before Luke lost control. That and Luke tapped the folder's edge against his palm hard enough to cut through his hand.

"I would appreciate any help you could provide in this matter. Discreet and limited to us only," David said.

Luke nodded. "Of course."

"The fewer people who know about this the better. There could be difficult repercussions. Questions I can't answer, which will only lead to more scrutiny."

Caleb was surprised it took this long to get to the politician-speak part of the talk. He liked David, thought the man might actually be what he seemed. But the whiff of power surrounding the man turned Caleb off. Big office, people scurrying to do his bidding, perks based on his title. To Caleb, a man should have to earn respect and not simply demand it because of his office.

"What you mean is we shouldn't talk to anyone about this," he said.

"Correct." David stood up, signaling the end of the meeting. "I would insist, however, to be kept in the loop."

Luke seemed to take the hint and got up, too. "Agreed."

"I bet you're sorry your former boss disbanded the Recovery Project now." Caleb couldn't resist the jab. To him the answer was so simple. The world needed groups like Recovery for assignments just like this.

"Actually no. It occurs to me you may be able to get a lot more done while working outside the law."

AVERY WAITED UNTIL A bus rattled by before she said anything. The meeting in the office fifteen minutes earlier still played in her mind. The buzz of people and traffic on Independence Avenue outside the Rayburn Building helped to bring her back to reality.

"He wasn't what I expected." Not that she'd ever met an almost-politician before. She'd been interviewed by prominent attorneys and met with clients whose lives were fodder for the news. Politicians were new.

"I'm reserving judgment." Caleb leaned against the white marble wall. They stood on the sidewalk but out of the direct path of tourists and congressional staffers bustling around them.

"He brought you guys in." She almost said "us" but stopped herself just in time. Whether she could play an integral role in Recovery was up to them. She was shocked at how much she wanted that answer to be yes.

Caleb didn't look impressed. "David could be setting us up."

She guessed a hearty dose of disbelief came with the job, but still. "Are you always so skeptical?"

"I learned that the hard way." He threw away the line without looking at her.

Luke frowned. "Damn, Caleb."

"What?" His head came up. When his gaze locked on hers, his eyes widened. "I didn't mean—"

Of course he did. She ignored the sharp pain and continued. "I have a possible way for us to figure out if Maddie Timmons is alive."

"How?" The frustration hadn't left Luke's voice when he asked the question.

She blocked it all out. Caleb, them, last night. It had all been a huge mistake, but none of that mattered except finding Maddie. "My contingency plan."

"Explain." Caleb's order didn't leave room for refusal.

"I set up a computer program that would send a copy of the test results, without any biographical information, to a private mail place. The instructions were to print it out and put it in my box."

Caleb pushed off from the wall. "And you're just mentioning this now?"

"It can't be used as evidence because there's no identi-

fiable information. Heck, unless the person who reads it
has a science background, they won't even understand
what they're seeing, but it can tell us if she was still
alive when Rod disappeared." She glanced around to
make sure none of the people passing by had stopped
to eavesdrop. They didn't, but she lowered her voice
anyway.

Now they had her paranoid.

"It's a fallback in case Adam can't find what he needs
on her." She directed her final comment to Caleb. "And
I didn't mention it before because I doubt it worked. I
tried to bypass internal security by making it look like
a personal email, but I don't know."

Caleb's smile appeared out of nowhere. "It worked."

His odd good mood confused her almost as much
as his sudden support. He morphed from indifferent
to angry to charming in the span of five minutes. She
never thought of him as prickly or temperamental. A
little irritable and maybe dark, but following the swings
now gave her a headache. "Why do you say that?"

"You're not someone who fails at things."

Analyzing the comment was out of the question. If
she started thinking it meant something, that he'd finally found something positive about her outside of the
bedroom, she'd only be disappointed.

She pretended she hadn't heard it. "Everything had
to fall our way for this to be an option. The testing had
to be finished on time and before the attack at the lab.
Damon had to miss the extra coding in the file. The
email had to work. The place had to get my instructions
right. Just don't get your hopes up."

"I'm betting you were successful. I'll be surprised if you weren't." Caleb turned to Luke. "We'll take her back to the warehouse and then go check it out."

She knew that was coming. Cutting her out under the guise of keeping her safe would appeal to two overly protective males. "Not going to work. I have to be there and sign."

"You used your own name?"

The soft tone to Caleb's voice didn't fool her. He was laying a verbal trap, and she had no intention of falling into it. "I didn't leave a paper trail, if that's what you're asking. Paid cash and asked that the box be listed anonymously. Everything goes by a number, not a name."

"I'm convinced," Luke said. "I'll go relieve Adam and send him to West Virginia to set up surveillance on the Timmons woman, or I guess I should say on the woman we hope is Maddie Timmons. You two head over to the mailbox place. In and out. Don't waste time."

Caleb started shaking his head before the words were out of Luke's mouth. "I don't like it."

"Me, either, but we have to get to the bottom of this disaster. If that DNA belongs to the Timmons woman, then she's dead and we have an imposter in West Virginia and someone to question. And if Timmons is alive, we need to keep her that way."

A bus pulled up beside them. Tourists carrying small flags and wearing matching blue T-shirts piled out of the door. They squealed and pointed. Cameras flashed. Two ladies insisted the Air and Space Museum was really the Capitol.

Caleb looked ready to bolt. If he did, she was going with him.

"What if Avery walks right into danger?" Caleb asked in a harsh whisper.

She put out her hand and pulled him out of the way before a kid with a skateboard ran him down. "You'll be there to help."

Luke slapped Caleb on the back. "You heard the lady. She's depending on you for protection."

"I guess you win." Caleb looked down at where her hand rested on his forearm. "This time."

Chapter Ten

Caleb didn't like the look of the place. It wasn't a big-name store. More of a mom-and-pop place if mom and pop were serial killers. It sat in a rundown strip mall in Northeast D.C. The bars on the windows, empty offices on one side and a self-storage business on the other weren't exactly welcoming. Neither was the deserted side street.

"How did you pick this location?" he asked, tensing for an answer that would drive him crazy.

"I wanted something that wasn't too obvious."

"What about safe? Did that criterion ever occur to you?"

She rolled her eyes at him as she slammed the car door. "It's not a prison."

"It's looks like a place prison escapees would go to hide." He toyed with the idea of making her wait in the car. He could go in and get out without ever putting her in danger. But when he realized he hadn't seen a car drive by since they parked, he wondered if the empty lot was any safer. Holding her gave him leverage. Also gave her a shield if she needed one.

He'd never been one to ignore his instincts. They were shouting at him to put her in the car and speed away. Zach lived for this sort of thing. The more remote and spooky, the better. Caleb could bring him back here to help.

There were just too many coincidences in this situation for his liking. When he took her to the lab, they were waiting. When she came to his house, they followed. He still wasn't sure who "they" were or how they got paid. Adam was working on that piece. But Caleb knew the men who kept coming for Avery were to be put down on sight.

Caleb tried to calculate the probability they knew to stake this site out, too.

Keys appeared under his nose. "Number eighty-one."

When he focused on the jingling, he noted her smile and the way she shook the chain in front of him. "Excuse me?"

"That's what we're looking for."

"If I asked you to stay—"

The smile didn't falter, but some of its light faded. "No."

It was worth a shot. Of course he could insist or even dump her in the car, but a scene was not the best idea. Then there was the issue of her determination. It ran bone deep. If she wanted something, she went for it. From the hands on her hips and lifted chin, he guessed she wanted whatever was in that mailbox pretty badly.

Since he didn't doubt her competence to handle rough

situations or his ability to protect her, he let it drop. "You heard Luke. We go in, check the box and go."

"I didn't plan to eat lunch here."

"Aren't you witty this afternoon?"

She let the keys drop in his hand. "I didn't get much sleep last night."

It was the first time she broached the subject. By the time he woke up this morning, she was in the kitchen talking with Zach. All signs of their lovemaking, the discarded clothes and sheets on only one bed, had been covered. "Are you complaining?"

"No."

And her honesty. It was as reliable as her spirit. He'd always found that refreshing. "Good."

"Just good?"

He had to wink at her then. "Mind-blowing."

"That's better."

He was sure it was his imagination, but her hips seemed to swing a little more when she walked. Since he spent a great deal of time looking at her butt, he noticed the difference. What he questioned was the reason for the change. The sex part was obvious, but this went beyond the physical. She no longer tensed when they were together as if waiting for him to land a verbal punch so she could do the same. Which was good since he no longer wanted to.

She walked up the steps to the store. At the top, she stopped and called to him over her shoulder. "You coming?"

"Wouldn't miss it."

He held out his arm and pushed the door open in front

of her. A small bell clanged. Not that the employees needed a warning of visitors. One stood behind a long wooden counter. The other fiddled with the paper tray on the copier. Both stared at the entrance and didn't pretend not to.

Two men in their thirties, both fit with matching military haircuts. Neither of those factors was incriminating on its own, but a warning siren rang in his head. He'd seen every man they killed. The description matched these two without fail.

The fact the one by the cash register kept a hand out of sight didn't make him guilty. Didn't make him innocent either.

"May we help you?" The man's voice sounded sincere and Southern. The only break from his neutral welcome was the way he looked Avery up and down.

Caleb thought about shooting the guy. If he didn't have an only-shoot-confirmed-bad-guys rule, he might have done it. Something sleazy rolled off this guy. Uniform or not, he seemed out of place.

"Just checking a mailbox." Avery slipped her hand through Caleb's arm.

He thought she was sending a silent signal of being taken until he realized she had tugged him in the direction of the boxes on the far right wall. While she scanned the rows for the right number, he focused on his peripheral vision and keeping the other men in it. He had a gun tucked at just the right angle in her bag for easy access and another by his ankle. The long-sleeve oxford hid a knife that he could throw almost as fast as he could shoot.

The guy at the counter cleared his throat. "I'm afraid you have to sign in before I can let you open that."

Avery didn't stop trailing her fingers down the row until she hit the right number. "Why?"

"What?"

"I have the key." She raised Caleb's arm and showed the man her proof dangling from Caleb's fingers. "It's my box."

The so-called employee spun a book around on the counter to face them. "Those are the rules. You sign and I compare your name to the name on file."

The guy was as subtle as being whacked with a stick. Either he thought he could sneak her phone number or he wanted to make sure he had the right prey. Caleb didn't like either option.

From his position, he could see the lines of writing on the pages, but that didn't make the supposed rule real. The writing could relate to anything. "I don't think—"

She stopped him by putting a hand on his chest. "It's okay."

That siren kept wailing in his brain, but he decided to trust her. When she slipped the key into his palm on her way to the desk, he knew she had a plan. He just wished she'd clued him in.

"You got this?" The second man, the one who didn't bother to check them out or say a word, set what looked like a printer part on the counter. "I need to head out."

"Sure."

With a nod in Caleb's general direction, the guy

slipped between Caleb and Avery and headed for the door. "Enjoy."

Caleb stationed his body in front of the mailbox. That gave him a clear shot of the door and whatever was happening at the counter. Caleb couldn't see the car or where the second guy went, but no matter where he stood, he'd have a blind spot. He did watch to make sure the man who left didn't lock them in. Last thing Caleb needed or wanted was a shoot-out in an office storefront.

Avery scribbled whatever name she'd used to set up the mailbox. If someone had traced the email from her office, it would only bring them to this building. The clerk had to match the false name Avery gave to an actual box. If this guy was dirty, he'd have the links he needed in about two seconds.

She glared at the box as she walked toward Caleb again. He assumed that meant she wanted it opened and now. As he put the key in the slot, he heard the scrape. Metal against wood. He recognized it, analyzed it and prepared for it, all in the span of time it took for him to breathe in.

In one fluid motion he reached out for her with one arm and for the gun by his shoe with the other. The keys clanked as they fell against the floor. His sneakers squeaked as he pivoted, pushing her behind him. The weapon molded to his palm as he spun around and aimed for the spot where the man last stood. The movements blurred together as he shifted and turned with crackling speed.

Avery's gasp echoed in his ear, but Caleb concentrated

all his energy on the other man. The one with the advantage. The one now pointing his weapon right at Caleb's head. That made two of them. The standoff, just feet apart, guaranteed instant death. The only question was who first.

"Drop it or I'll shoot her." The man was smart enough to see his opportunity and took it.

Caleb didn't move except to put his body that much closer to hers. "Who are you working for?"

"This isn't question-and-answer time."

"You're going to shoot an innocent woman?" Caleb knew the guy would probably shoot his own mother for the right price.

"You're wasting your time with guilt."

Caleb was stalling, assessing his opponent and checking for weaknesses. "What will work?"

"You have two seconds to obey."

There was that word. He hated it. Reacted to it whenever someone used it around him. "You're as likely to die as I am."

"Are you willing to take the chance with her life?"

Caleb felt her fingers at his back small and almost imperceptible. She wasn't tugging or acting like a desperate woman on the brink of death. Not his Avery. She was pressing something against him. Hard and loaded, it was the one something that could shift the odds to their side—his second gun.

The idea of putting her in danger landed like a kick to his chest. But when she jabbed him with his own weapon, he knew she wouldn't be denied. If they were going down, they were going down shooting.

"You've got one second left," the other man said.

"Okay." Caleb lifted his fingers off the gun, holding his hands out in what he hoped looked like surrender. "Just don't shoot."

"Enough talking. Put the weapon on the floor."

Caleb nodded but didn't move.

"Ma'am?" The man wiggled a finger at her. "You come over here with me so your boyfriend doesn't try anything stupid."

Caleb put his hand out to the side to block that from happening. The only way he could win this thing was if he knew she was out of firing range. In front of him she could get caught in the cross fire. "She stays here."

"You're not in charge." The guy frowned. "I said on the floor."

No way was that going to happen. "I'm going."

"While you're at it, lie down and put your hands over your head."

"Anyone could come in." Avery's voice never wavered as she drew the other man's attention. It was as if a settled calm had washed over her.

The guy's smirk was immediate. "Wrong."

He might be good with a gun but his ego got in his way. Almost always happened. Keep an attacker talking and he'd tell you the one thing he didn't want you to know. Caleb now suspected the second guy was outside in a lookout position. They had two, not one, enemies to get through.

"Now, boyfriend. Get moving. On the floor, and I'm not going to say it again. The next time, I shoot your leg and we'll see you drop."

Caleb let his knees bend as he slid his gun onto the floor. The timing had to be perfect. There would be a split second when the guy eased his stance, when he believed he'd disarmed the bigger threat, and focused his attention on Avery instead.

Easing down a few inches, Caleb started toward the floor as ordered. He bent over slightly, trying to block the other man's view, and reached back. Avery shoved the second gun in his hand. At the same time, he felt something slip out of his waistband, from under his shirt. Swinging his arm as he stood, Caleb fired his shot. The air stilled as he waited for a return hit and shifted to the side for a better shot. There wasn't a need. The guy slammed against the wall as blood dripped from his forehead. His gun thudded on the counter as he slid to the floor.

Caleb took in the open eyes and mouth. It was another moment before he noticed the knife sticking out of the guy's chest. Not a direct hit to the heart, but a wound that would have stopped him. Would have saved them.

Avery. Caleb spun around and saw her, arm still extended, staring at the horror in front of her.

"Damn, woman." His whisper carried a mix of pride and concern.

"I did it."

"You okay?"

"He's dead."

"Very." Caleb lowered her hand and pulled her into his arms, letting his warmth calm the violent shaking of her body.

Stiff and still, she stood wrapped in his arms. She

didn't cling or return the touch. He almost wished she would cry or scream. Something to let the emotions out. With the lab gone as a buffer, she had to face this side of death. The real side.

He tried to tell himself the hug was for her. In reality, he needed it as much as she did. In those crucial minutes when he formulated his plan, only one goal stuck in his mind. He had to save her. And she was fine. He repeated that over and over as he brought her to the side and out of the line of sight of the front door. If there was a second gunman out there, and he suspected there was, Caleb didn't want the guy to have an easy shot.

When he tried to pull away, to trick his brain into wanting something other than the comfort of her body, she grabbed hold of him. Fingers grabbed at his shirt as she buried her face in his neck.

Aftermath. It flooded through her, shaking her hard enough to rattle her teeth.

He brushed his lips over her ear and across her forehead. Anything to soothe and calm her. "I know, baby."

"I thought he'd kill you as soon as you laid down the gun. The knife was the only thing I could think to do."

"You did great."

"I was scared to death."

"You think I wasn't?" Terrified, panicked. All the words fit. Caleb had never worried about his life. He lived by the theory that if it was his time, he would accept it without regrets. Gambling with *her* life was not a game he wanted to play.

She snorted. "You don't get scared."

The woman had no clue. The key was to conquer the fear and let it fuel the fight. "We need to grab that paper and get out of here."

She stared at him for an extra beat and then nodded. Stepping back, she picked up the key and went to the box. She tried to unlock it. It took her three tries to get the key in the slot, and she only then managed it when Caleb held her hand steady.

She clenched the document in her fist while he watched the door. Nothing moved outside. He waited for cars to go by or the other man to appear. The sound of gunfire should have gotten the guy's attention, should have brought someone running. All the scenarios Caleb ran in his head didn't happen. Hard to imagine the dead attacker worked alone, but it was possible.

"I'm ready."

Her shaky smile said otherwise, but he let it go. When she headed for the front of the office, he shook his head. "Through the back."

"You don't think it's over."

"I know it's not."

Chapter Eleven

If Caleb was trying to scare her, he was doing a fine job of it. She'd just gotten her legs to stop wobbling. The only thing keeping food in her stomach was her refusal to glance in the dead man's direction.

Avery didn't regret the knife or the gun. The man behind the counter had made it clear he planned to take Caleb out and do heaven knew what with her. He was one in a long line of bad guys sent after her. In a battle of them versus her, she wanted to win. With Caleb she could.

He leaned over the slumped body, searching in his pockets and checking for a pulse. Then he scanned the shelves behind the counter and picked up the phone, only to hang it right back up again.

When his gaze went to the ceiling, she gave in to her curiosity. "What are you doing?"

"He didn't have any identification."

"And you thought he might have thrown it up in the air?" She didn't fight the sarcasm that crept into her voice.

"I'm looking for cameras, anything that will lead us back to this guy's boss."

Caleb had a reason for everything he did. No wasted motion or random thoughts. He analyzed a scene and acted. There was a huge comfort in seeing him work. "Makes sense. See any?"

"There." He pointed to the far corner. "The light is off. This guy likely disabled them."

"No question they're pros."

"None."

"I may never sleep again."

"I can probably help you with any bedroom problems you may have." Caleb held out his hand. "Come on. We're leaving."

She didn't argue. Being in the same room with a dead guy made her dizzy, even if she'd seen death. When she was fourteen she found her mother dead of a heart attack in the middle of the kitchen. One minute she came rushing in the door to share her news about making the field hockey team. The next she was on her knees rocking back and forth while the emergency operator shouted CPR instructions.

The memory of that moment stuck with her. She knew this one would, too.

Caleb crowded in front of her as they walked sideways to the back of the store. Every few seconds, he would glance over her shoulder at the front door, keeping every entrance covered.

On one side of the short hallway was a small empty bathroom. The other had a door marked Storeroom. He motioned for her to stand to the side. He counted on his fingers then threw open the door. From her vantage, she couldn't see inside, but whatever was in there had him lowering his gun.

His breathing slowed and his mouth set in a grim line. "We're too late here."

"What?" She got a quick peek inside before he pulled her back. She saw the outline of two bodies, male and partially undressed, and that was enough. "Who are they?"

"Probably the real clerks."

Guilt slammed into her from every direction. She did this. She brought evil to this store and cost those men their lives.

"Don't." Caleb brushed his fingertips down her cheek. "Don't take this on."

"But I—"

"Sent an email." Caleb nodded in the direction of the front room. "This is his crime, not yours."

She didn't trust her voice. Leaning into Caleb's hand, she nodded.

"Wait here." He stepped into the room before she could grab him. After a quick check of the bodies, he shuffled through the shelves and stopped at a black box. The top opened.

"What is it?"

"It should be the security tape, but it's gone."

Looked as if nothing was going to go their way. "Like I said, pros."

"We'll call Luke as soon as we're in the car." Caleb closed the door and put a hand on the small of her back.

With gentle pressure, he guided her toward the back door at the end of the hall.

"You think someone is out there."

"There were two bodies in that room. Two missing uniforms. With our one dead guy out front, the guy who left must be waiting somewhere nearby." Caleb's face closed up. "The worst part is I let him get by me. He walked right out of the store."

"Now who's taking responsibility for everyone else's actions?"

He dropped a quick kiss on her mouth and was gone before she could pull him closer. "There are probably a million places to hide outside and only a few ways for us to escape."

She couldn't fault his logic. She just wanted him to be wrong. There'd been enough death for one day. She wanted a shower and a long, deep sleep in Caleb's arms. Getting her life back would be a big plus, but she doubted that would happen anytime soon...if ever.

Again, he positioned his body between her and potential danger. He walked out first, gun ready and gaze scanning the area.

Knowing he didn't need her fighting him, she only followed when he motioned her outside. The alley smelled like spoiled food. Other than stacks of trash-cans and cardboard boxes, there was nothing much back there.

He shook his head. "This doesn't make sense."

She had no idea what gnawed at him. Her mind wouldn't focus long enough for her to think the situation through. "Can we keep going?"

When his gaze met hers, the harsh lines on his face softened. "Yeah."

In double time they headed around the side of the building, past the empty store next to the mail place. His head never stopped moving and his weapon never wavered. They ducked back against the wall when a lone car passed by the road, then they walked again.

The front of the building looked the same as when they went inside. There was a car in a space perpendicular to the building and theirs was in the space down about thirty feet from the front door.

She pressed her back against the cool cement wall. "Maybe he left?"

Caleb shook his head. "Not likely."

The back of her neck itched. She guessed it was her mind playing games, but she felt as if someone was staring at her. Assessing and waiting. Hanging out with Caleb and the rest of the agents did that to her. Made her question everything and everyone. She wasn't sure how they lived that way, but she didn't fight the effectiveness.

She scanned the line of trees on the far side of the lot. "Hiding?"

"That's my guess."

"So, what's the plan?"

He leaned a hand against the wall next to her head. "A decoy."

From this position, if anyone saw their whispered conversation, they would assume intimacy. The way he leaned in, pressing his chest against hers. The way he never broke eye contact.

"Meaning?" she asked.

"I'm going to walk out there."

There were only two options and she knew he wouldn't nominate her, but still. "Absolutely not."

He bent his elbow and crowded in closer. "You want to keep standing here?"

"Call for backup."

"Zach is on the way, but I don't want him shot either." He reached into her bag.

"What are you doing?"

"Getting some supplies." Caleb pulled out a small lens.

She'd never seen it before, so she did a quick check to see what else she'd missed. "When did you put that in there?"

"On the way out of the warehouse."

"Resourceful."

He aimed the lens at the trees then swept across the parking lot to the side closest to them. "It's one of my skills."

"One of them, yes. See anything?"

"No."

"So, it's safe?"

He hesitated. "Stay behind me, head tucked, hands on me, and I mean stuck to me so that I can't tell where I end and you begin. Got that?"

"Yes."

"You hear footsteps or gunfire, you get into that car and drive. Do not look back."

"I'm not leaving without you."

He placed the keys in her palm and folded her fingers

over them. "Tell me you agree or we don't move. And keep in mind the longer we stand here, the more likely we are to become victims."

"That's low."

"I'm serious."

She tightened her hand on the bag over her shoulder. "Caleb."

"Avery."

The man defined stubborn. "Fine."

He started moving. They stayed close to the building with her back to the wall and shuffled from post to post, tucking behind each and trying to keep out of sight. Nothing could get to her. An attacker would have to get through one of two immovable objects to reach her. She bet Caleb would be tougher than the thick inches of wood and steel.

When they'd gone as far as they could and remain under the building's awning, he stopped her. Any further movement would expose them. Keeping her behind the post, he held her an arm's length away. With careful footsteps he walked away from her and slipped to the front of the post.

She knew he was trying to draw fire by sacrificing his body for hers. She didn't want a martyr. She pushed away from the safety and flattened against him again, ignoring his string of whispered profanity.

"We do this together," she said.

He didn't respond, but he did start sliding around the post. They got the whole way to the front of the car without anything happening. No one jumped out or fired. They didn't have to duck for cover. But Caleb didn't ease up. Every muscle vibrated with alertness. His gun fit in his hand as though he was born with it there.

She lifted her hand and aimed the automatic door opener at the car. Before she could hit the button, he batted her hand down.

"Wait." His attention went to the ground.

"What is it?" She followed his gaze. The sandy area around the car door was pristine. No clues that she could see.

Something about the site struck her as wrong, but she couldn't say what. She followed a visual path around the front of the car and then to the back. There, near the rear tire, was a partial footprint.

The answer hit her. There should have been more. Hers and his. The place had been wiped clean while they were inside. She couldn't figure out why that would happen.

Caleb pulled her with him toward the side of the building as he screamed the word "Run!"

They got ten racing steps before the ground shook and a thundering boom shrieked in her ears. An invisible wall of air pressed against her back. Her bag was ripped off her arm as a wave of heat engulfed her.

She tried to focus but the trees blurred in front of her and her feet left the ground. The force pushing from behind her didn't stop. The air left her lungs as she slammed against the dirt on her knees. Momentum shoved her head into the ground. She tried to lift her head but the world spun and her neck grew heavy.

She heard Caleb yell her name right before the world went dark.

Chapter Twelve

Trevor hung up the phone. Listening to the excitement threading through Russell's voice ruined Trevor's day. The man rambled on about how he'd taken out Avery Walker. About how it could never be traced back to him and would look like an accident with the fuel line.

A car bomb. Talk about not being subtle.

Russell actually bragged about killing one of the Recovery agents. Trevor couldn't see Russell strutting around, chest puffed out and mouth smug, but he heard it. The man acted as if he'd achieved something impossible and brilliant. As if this was a *good* thing.

The idiot.

There were men you did not want as enemies. The Recovery agents definitely qualified. Not too long ago Trevor had made a deal with Luke. Trevor couldn't think of another person, another group of men, he would have forgiven for the death of his brother. The reluctant respect ran deep.

When Trevor made the hands-off promise, he intended to keep it. Russell's actions threatened that tenuous stand-down. If Recovery got even a whiff of

Trevor's involvement with Russell and the death of one of their own, they'd be relentless in their pursuit. His company, his security, even his freedom would be threatened. He had power, but they would die for their cause. It was hard to win a battle against people who had nothing left to lose.

Recovery would come hard and lethal and not stop until they wiped out the people responsible for killing their fellow agent. And eliminating an innocent woman? That was one of those things Luke and his crowd would never accept. They would dig until they uncovered every last participant in the WitSec scam. Dig and destroy.

Trevor hadn't wanted to get involved. He'd hoped Russell would piss off the wrong person and suddenly disappear. The chances were good. The man worked completely without boundaries. Smart but dangerous in his belief of his infallibility. Men like him always met with a quick and nasty downfall. It was just a question of who would hand it to him.

Trevor had created the trail to point all fingers back to Russell should anyone figure out how to access the WitSec computers or Russell's personal files. Trevor laid all the groundwork so that as soon as he tracked down the incriminating tape, he could sit back and wait for Russell's crushing blow.

Russell had ruined the timing. Now Trevor had to move faster than anticipated.

The only way to end this, to protect his behind-the-scenes assistance, was to hand Russell over to Recovery. Trevor would have to erase any lines or hint of a connection between him and Russell. The conspiracy would begin and end with Russell. That's what Luke would find. Everyone involved in this mess would be satisfied and safe. Those who benefited could collect their cash and then find a new scheme.

Except Russell. The dead didn't need cover.

Trevor picked up the phone. He'd need his best men on this. The Recovery agents wouldn't be easy to track. They were experienced in losing tails and experts in hiding their tracks. But Trevor needed to know where they were at all times. The only way to battle them was on an even field. That meant he could lose more of his men. For Russell's sake, that better not happen.

THE CLUNKING WOULDN'T stop. It was as though a huge metal press kept clamping down in Avery's head. It smashed and thumped. But that was the good part. The pain pinging around the inside of her skull was the worst.

She sensed the lights were on. The ground underneath her was hard and flat. She inhaled, trying to pick up the smells of that awful alley and orient her mind, but the scent was more familiar. Then the muffled voices around her grew more distinct. They went from rumbling in the background to…loud and yelling.

"Caleb, sit down."

She recognized Luke's shout and the soft hum of the machines from the warehouse. That quick the tension eased from her shoulders and the hammering in her head slowed its beat. The light touch of fingers against her forehead contrasted with the tight grip on her hand.

"Well?"

She'd know that demanding tone anywhere. Caleb. She struggled to open her eyes.

"She's awake," a female voice whispered.

"Finally."

Two women. Their voices swirled around her, coming from near her feet. It was a strange event in a house full of men. There was only one explanation.

"Mia and Claire?" Avery asked.

Someone squeezed her hand. "Wake up."

Only Caleb would issue an order like that. Even though Avery dreaded the shock of light, she slowly opened her eyes. The ceiling beams came into focus. She saw a flash of the room and then Caleb's face moved right in front of her.

"About time." He hovered, his face pale and his mouth turned down. He managed to look furious, relieved and terrible all at the same time.

She touched her fingertips to his cheek. "You smell like smoke."

"You look like hell."

"How romantic."

"We came within inches of being barbecued." If possible, his mouth turned down even farther. "Zach did recon on the bomb and brought back the pieces. I called in a favour with the authorities for the rest."

"Bomb?"

"Zach's our explosives expert."

"But where?"

"Under the car. Remotely detonated."

The harsh scratch of Caleb's voice and pained expression made her think the worst. She did a mental head count of the voices she'd heard. The idea was to figure out who was missing from the room. "Did someone die?"

"You almost did." His husky voice sounded deeper than usual.

"Don't be an idiot. She did not." Luke shoved Caleb to the side. "How's the head?"

She raised her free hand and felt a bandage. "What happened?"

"You don't remember?"

The bang and the heat. The fire. She bolted straight up and grabbed for the hand that had been holding hers. "Where's Caleb?"

"Still right here." That fast he was at her side again.

All the people in the room came into focus, but she concentrated on him. "Are you okay?"

"Fine."

She struggled to sit up and would have fallen back down on the conference table except for his arm around her shoulder. The world flip-flopped as her vision blurred. For a second she thought she'd blow that throw-up record, but then the room stilled.

The women crowded in front of her on each side of Luke. They were like light and dark. Both had long hair but in different shades. She knew them from their photos in the paper, but the grainy images didn't capture the energy that bounced off them. Mia reminded Avery of sunshine, while Claire radiated pure sultry heat. Beautiful with matching looks of concern.

"I thought we'd never meet. This is a heck of a way

to do it." As careful as possible, Avery glanced between them.

Claire smiled. "Luke eased up on his house restrictions when he heard about the explosion. I have a one-hour reprieve. I'm sure he'll be hustling me back home in a few minutes."

Luke nodded. "And it's over. Holden should be back any second."

"I thought I heard a clock ticking."

"Claire." The warning was clear in Luke's tone.

"What?" She threw her arms wide. "Everyone is here. We're perfectly safe."

Luke glared at his wife's stomach. "You get sick every ten minutes right now."

"Don't remind me."

Avery had so many questions and so much she needed to say to Caleb, but there was a protocol to these types of things. And Claire's happiness was contagious. "Congratulations on the baby. That's wonderful news."

From her interactions with Luke, Avery knew he would be a terrific father. Strong and protective and so obviously in love with his wife. When Claire smiled, he smiled. Even when he glared at her, a sparkle in his eyes said he enjoyed the male-female battle. That he would shatter if he lost her.

"We're thrilled." Claire's hand went to her still-flat abdomen.

Not for the first time, Avery thought about Claire's past and wondered how she'd ever made it to this point. She and Luke had overcome so much. They survived a monster and put aside their troubled past.

It gave Avery hope. Maybe Caleb could learn from Luke's example. If she could figure out a way to take the heat between them and spin it into something deeper, Caleb might look at her as if she mattered to his future. That was the dream, but in looking at Mia and Claire's smiling faces, Avery realized dreams do sometimes come true.

Luke frowned at her. "Avery, you should rest. You're banged up and have a gash over your eye."

"That explains the killer headache."

Caleb bent down and slipped his arm under her legs. "I'm taking you to the hospital."

"Stop." Luke held out a hand and kept it there until Caleb put her back down on the table. "The injury is nothing serious. A nuisance only. You know that."

Caleb grunted. At least she thought that's what the noise was. It was hard to tell since he didn't stand up again. He leaned against her, his weight almost crushing her. If his warmth hadn't felt so good she would have asked him to loosen his hold.

"You two were lucky today. The attackers had a plan and a backup. If that second guy had stuck around after throwing the switch..." Luke stared up at the ceiling.

Avery was grateful he stopped. She didn't want to think about what could have happened. What did happen was bad enough. "Don't feel lucky at the moment, but tomorrow might be better."

Luke laughed. "I bet. Sleep and we'll debrief you later."

"Of course you're not going to question her now. She

needs to recover first." The outrage in Claire's voice almost made Avery laugh.

Luke didn't seem as amused. "Didn't I just say that?"

The love between Luke and Claire overrode their bickering. Anyone watching closely could see it. Avery envied the closeness, the comfort in knowing you could argue with someone and not lose them.

She turned to the one man she thought could give her that. "Are you okay?"

"Fine."

"I think we should check on Caleb's leg."

Avery hadn't even noticed Zach until he spoke up. He stood at one end of the conference table with his arms folded over his chest. The frown he sent Caleb didn't look too promising.

Neither did Caleb's reaction. "I said no."

She caught Zach's quick glance in the direction of Caleb's feet. When Zach did it a second time, Avery knew something was going on. Zach acted with an economy of movement. Everything he did or said had a purpose and a worried frown replaced the blank expression he usually wore.

"Prove it. Walk around," Zach said.

"Let it go." Caleb's voice shook with anger.

His heated reaction was all out of proportion to the conversation. It took only a moment for her head to clear and instinct to kick in. Zach was trying to send a message, a subtle but necessary one.

"What's wrong?" she asked.

Zach hitched his chin at Caleb. "Him."

When she shifted to face Caleb, she threw off his balance. He slid off her and stumbled back. His feet tangled, but he put up his arms to prevent a fall. "I just need to sit."

Luke rushed forward and grabbed Caleb before he fell over backward. "What the—"

"Blood." Zach pointed. "His sneaker is soaked."

"I'm fine."

Panic flushed through Avery's veins as she looked down. Red stained Caleb's pants and the floor. Her gaze traveled up to his face. His cheeks where stark white.

"God, Caleb. It's everywhere."

"Fell on a rock. Not a big deal." Caleb panted out the words as his body slumped hard against Luke's.

"Zach. A little help here." Luke barely got the words out before Caleb hit the floor.

Chapter Thirteen

He'd passed out.

Caleb remembered hearing Avery's voice and watching everyone scramble toward him. Then his mind went blank and his knees gave out. He'd been injured at the Academy and a bunch of times playing sports while growing up. Even been grazed by a bullet and stabbed in his shoulder. Through all that he'd never passed out.

This was worse than all those other times. There were witnesses. Many of them. Caleb was secure enough not to be embarrassed, but the minute he woke up he'd promised to shoot anyone who made a joke. No one dared.

He leaned back on the beat-up sofa under the warehouse stairs. With his head resting against the cushions, the room didn't spin as fast. Shame he couldn't find anything to stop the pain pulsing in his knee. Resting it on the coffee table wasn't helping. Neither did the ice around the swelling or the medication.

Seventeen stitches and a tetanus shot. His knee looked like a map now.

Definitely not his best day.

He closed his eyes. "What the hell did Luke give me?"

"Painkiller," Zach said.

"I can't stay awake."

Zach chuckled. "That's the point."

"I need to check on Avery." The only thing keeping Caleb on the couch was the knowledge she was fine. After Luke worked on his knee and everyone cleared out, Avery and Zach stayed behind. Zach had even stayed the night in case Avery needed his help.

Avery. She'd fussed over him and helped him wash up without getting his new stitches wet. If her hands hadn't felt so good traveling all over his body and washing his hair, he might have insisted on privacy.

Not that he wanted to be away from her. Not anymore.

Almost losing her shifted his priorities. The woman he thought he knew, the one who tossed him aside to get a promotion, was not the woman in front of him now. This Avery used the same determination in her private life that she did at work. She didn't back down from a challenge or sacrifice others to save herself.

It was hard to take it all in. He couldn't figure out if he'd been wrong or she had changed. He wasn't even sure he cared about which one turned out to be right.

"She's been in the shower for a long time, hasn't she?" He lifted his head and listened for the water.

"For a guy who professes to be over Avery, you sure act like you want to be under her."

Caleb stopped staring at the ceiling and focused on Zach. He hadn't moved. He'd sat in the same chair for hours, elbows resting on his knees and staring at Caleb as if willing him to get well. From anyone else the move would have been weird. For Zach it seemed spooky but normal. He had a grounded sense of loyalty. There was no one more quietly dependable. Caleb knew if he asked Zach to sit there all night he would.

"Have you heard me use the word 'over' since I brought her here?"

Zach smiled. "Nope."

"Okay then."

"Haven't heard you apologize to her either."

There was a difference between forgiving Avery and forgetting everything that had passed between them. Only an idiot would do the latter. "For what?"

"You tell me."

"I was blindsided by what she did back then."

"Any chance you had tunnel vision?"

Caleb felt his temper flare. It wasn't like Zach to butt in to other people's lives. Certainly wasn't his usual style to question people's motives. "Meaning?"

"Just throwing the thought out there."

Caleb was too tired to dissect Zach's secret code. "It's not as simple as you think."

"Never is when women are involved."

"How's the patient?" Avery asked as she descended the stairs.

Zach smiled. "Arguing, so you tell me."

"Sounds normal to me."

Caleb blocked out the joking and concentrated on the walking. Watching her move was just about the sexiest thing he'd ever seen. The sweats and T-shirt Mia dropped off hid most of Avery's best assets. But her face, scrubbed clean and shiny, and that big smile had him holding his breath. Even the bandage highlighted her beauty.

She sat down next to him and slid her hand over his good thigh. "How are you feeling?"

"Better."

The casual way she touched him, as if it was the most natural thing in the world, filled him with a deep sense of satisfaction. Just two weeks ago he'd vowed to wipe her from his memory and find a woman worth having.

She glanced over at Zach. "Is he lying?"

Zach nodded. "Little bit."

Caleb wasn't about to discuss the jabbing pains running up and down his leg. Avery finally had relaxed and found her smile. It took two hours after he woke up for her to stop biting her bottom lip, and another hour for the color to return to her cheeks. Seeing her like that hurt more than his injury. No way was he inviting a second round.

But he couldn't deny he enjoyed having her play nursemaid. When he couldn't drag his body to the bathroom, he decided against climbing the stairs to go to bed. She immediately went into action. She had Luke and Zach drag the mattress down so they could sleep on the bottom floor. He tossed. He turned. She stayed with him all night.

"What time does Vince get here?" Caleb asked, hoping to change the subject.

Avery frowned. "Who?"

He slipped his arm along the back of the sofa and let

his fingers tangle in her damp hair. "Vince Ritter. He's with us."

"You hired someone else? Another agent?" She looked appalled at the idea. "Exactly how long did I sleep?"

This close he could smell her shampoo. Something coconut. He guessed that was Mia's doing, as well. She'd appointed herself Avery's caretaker, and Caleb appreciated the generosity.

"He's Rod's former partner. They worked WitSec together."

She squeezed his thigh. "And?"

"Vince has been helping out," Zach said.

She snorted. "He's late."

"What?"

"Where was he when the car exploded?"

The red light next to the door flashed as a siren sounded on the computer panel. Zach got up and went to the monitor at the end of the row. "That's him."

Avery followed Zach, peeking over his shoulder at all the tech equipment. "Not what I expected."

Caleb picked up a strange tone. "What did you expect?"

"Don't know." She watched Zach type on the keyboard. "Vince doesn't have the code to get in?"

"Only Recovery agents have the code," Zach said.

She spun around to face Caleb. "You gave it to me."

"I made an exception."

She continued to stare at him while the huge steel door pressed open and rolled back.

Vince poked his head inside. "Everybody in one piece?"

"For now." Zach met Vince at the entrance and shook his hand.

"Didn't anyone tell you not to play with explosives?" Vince joked as he shook Caleb's hand.

"You'd think there would be a warning on the package about that sort of thing." Caleb tried to sit up before his slouch put him on the floor. "Avery, this is Vince."

"It's nice to finally meet you." Vince's hand closed over hers. "Even better to know you're okay."

"It will take more than a car bomb to knock her down." Caleb felt his chest fill with pride. He couldn't believe how strong she'd turned out to be. Forget her tendency to stick to the rules no matter what. He needed her to bend, and she did.

She snorted. "Didn't feel that way yesterday."

Vince leaned against the conference table. "Was it at least worth it?"

"No." Avery jumped in with her answer before either Caleb or Zach could talk.

Vince looked at all of them, moving his stare from one to the other before settling back at Avery again. "You didn't find anything?"

She shook her head and then stared Caleb down.

He gave the answer she appeared to want from him. "No."

Zach didn't react to the lie either. They both sat there, following her lead. Caleb had no idea what she was doing or why, but it seemed important to her that Vince not know the truth right now, so they conceded. There would be time for questions later.

Vince frowned. "The test results weren't there?"

"No." Avery moved over to the couch and sat on the arm just above Caleb. She didn't touch him or even give him a signal. She just sat there as if her presence should reassure him she had a plan.

Funny enough, it did. He figured he had two choices. He could step in and correct the record or he could trust her. Zach barely knew her and he didn't question her. He didn't make her prove her position or explain her reason.

It was a wake-up call. Caleb had made love to her more times than he could count, had raced all over the D.C. metro area with her trying to end this WitSec nightmare, and still he acted as if she owed him something.

That would end today. Whatever happened before was in the past. Today would start their future. Trust would build from here. She had earned that much from him.

"We did have some other things to worry about, but the box was empty," he said.

Vince's shoulders fell. "Then I'm afraid we're back at the beginning. We don't know anything and don't have any leads."

"At least we're not worse off." Zach finally spoke up but didn't expose Avery's ruse.

Caleb figured Avery didn't even realize she had dug her fingers into his forearm as she waited for Zach to speak. When he silently sided with her, she unclenched her grip.

Caleb wondered how long it would be before circulation returned to his hand. "Tell my knee that nothing's changed."

Vince turned to Zach. "You had something you wanted me to look at?"

"Adam has some questions about your replacement, Russell Ambrose."

"He's a good agent."

Zach swiveled his chair to face the monitors again. "He has a few oddities in his schedule."

"Meaning?"

"He was talking with Bram Walters right around the time this mess came down."

"To be fair, that could be anything. Might just be that Russell is the one Bram went to seeking inside information."

Zach tapped his pen against the screen. "Possibly. I need you to tell me if the communications look like the usual congressional inquiries."

Vince sighed and stood up. "Show me."

Caleb waited until Zach and Vince were busy studying lines of data to glance at Avery again. She continued to glare at Vince. This time the focus was on his back. Something about the older man ticked her off. Caleb could see it in every part of her body, her muscles tight and alert.

The reaction didn't make sense. Caleb had known Vince since throwing in with Recovery. The guy was solid. Not that Caleb had a huge number of dealings with him, but Rod and Vince remained close friends even after their work together ended. Vince had advised

Recovery on their communications and emergency strategies. He never actively participated in cases and they never provided him with confidential information, but he was an ear if they needed one.

Caleb wasn't angry with her reaction, but he couldn't help be curious. If this was a woman's-intuition thing, he wanted to know what vibe she picked up that he'd missed. Mia had that talent. Probably had something to do with her therapy background, but that woman could read a person better than anyone Caleb had ever met. Mia was using her skills and studying profiling. They all agreed Mia's insights would be valuable if they could gather more information. Right now there was nothing to show her because they didn't have a lead or a possible suspect now that Bram was gone.

Caleb lifted his head and smiled when she leaned down. Her nose almost touched his. Her pretty eyes narrowed. "What?"

"Want to tell me why we're lying to Vince?" Caleb whispered.

"I didn't mean to."

He almost laughed. "Yeah, you did."

"Well, sort of." She nibbled on her lip as her gaze traveled over to Vince one more time. The minute she focused on him, her shoulders straightened. "I don't know."

He didn't need a psychology degree or Mia's help to know Avery was stalling. He understood. It wasn't as if he made it easy for her to open up to him. Even after they had sex the other night, he shut her out. She wanted to talk and he wanted a mental breather as he tried to take in how his body reacted to hers.

Rather than kick and fuss, she accepted his coldness. It was as if she'd come to expect nothing more from him. That thought made him wish his leg had healed so he could kick his own butt.

"Avery?"

"It's nothing." She rubbed her palm up and down his arm as she talked.

He doubted she even realized she was touching him. "Tell me."

She tore her gaze away from Vince and stared down at Caleb. "You really want to know?"

"I trust your judgment."

Her head pulled back as if he'd slapped her. "Since when?"

Guilt rushed in at him. He'd done this to her, convinced her that her opinion meant nothing to him. Little did she know she was the only thing keeping him moving right now. Exhaustion threatened to take him down at any moment. Seeing her, fueling his energy off her seemingly endless supply, made the pain bearable on limited pain meds.

He tugged her down closer, until his mouth brushed over hers. "You're not the only one who's learned a few things, you know."

She barely moved. "Like what?"

This close he could see the rich brown of her eyes, smell the sweet scent of her skin. The temptation to forget the job and kick the other men out nearly overwhelmed him. The only way to stay focused was to make her talk.

He smiled. "Let's stick with one conversation at a time."

"You're sure?"

"Yeah."

She sighed. "Vince isn't part of the team."

She spoke so low he had to strain to hear her. "He's Rod's former partner."

"So?"

To Caleb that carried some weight. Didn't seem to impress Avery one bit, so he tried again. "He has knowledge and contacts that can help us with this."

"And?"

"Speaking from experience, it's hard to come up with a solid plan if you don't have the necessary basic information." His voice trailed off when she rolled her eyes. "What?"

"You're not listening."

"I'm not?"

She did a quick glance in Vince's direction. He hadn't moved. Whatever Zach was showing Vince kept him occupied. Knowing Zach, Caleb wouldn't be surprised if he deliberately pulled Vince into something as a way of assisting Avery.

She got up and circled to the other side of Caleb. She pressed up against his side with her hand on his chest. For a second he thought she was trying to divert his attention, then he realized she was putting her back to Vince as she lowered her voice even further.

Warm breath washed over his ear as she spoke. "Why didn't Rod go to him?"

"What?"

"If Rod and Vince were so close, why did Rod come to me?"

"Well, I'm sure…" Caleb actually couldn't come up with an explanation.

"It's not as if we met all the time or even talked at the beginning. I had only seen Rod a few times since you started with Recovery. One day, without warning, he showed up and asked for my help."

Caleb had wondered how Rod roped her into this dangerous situation. Now he knew. Rod had simply asked for help. He probably invoked Ryan's name as he did it. Avery would find that lure irresistible.

"You had the expertise with the DNA testing," Caleb suggested.

"But Rod has all those contacts."

"The same question could be asked about us." Caleb heard Vince laugh and glanced over at him. Seemed Avery's unreasonable anger was rubbing off because the sound ticked Caleb off. "Rod could have brought Recovery in and we'd have worked it as a team. He didn't."

"You hate that."

"I didn't say that."

"You didn't have to. It's only natural you'd be upset that he didn't come to you. You're a DNA specialist. You have the same expertise that I do."

He didn't realize how much it ticked him off until she said it in her matter-of-fact tone. "I know."

"Do you understand why he didn't turn to you?"

Caleb kept trying to block that question from his brain. If he didn't ask it, he didn't have to think about the real reason. "It doesn't matter."

"Caleb, don't shut me out." She brushed her thumb over his chin.

He kissed her fingers. "I'm not."

"Do not assume something that's not there. Rod was trying to protect you."

She was trying to console him. Caleb recognized it and reacted by sharing feelings he didn't even know he had. "Or he didn't trust us. Didn't think I could do it."

"He talked about all of you all the time. He was so proud. So convinced he'd assembled the best team anywhere." Those dark eyes were so soulful, so achingly sweet.

Caleb almost lost the thread of the conversation. "I get it."

"But you're still missing my main point."

"Which is?"

"Rod never mentioned Vince. You guys mattered. He didn't."

The words cut straight through Caleb. All those hours of wondering why Rod had made the choices he did and why he didn't check in came back to Caleb. He hadn't wanted to deal with it or admit it, but anger festered there. It came out in hatred for Bram and Trevor and frustration over losing the old Recovery program.

"Don't forget that part, Caleb."

He nodded because he didn't trust himself to say

anything. Thanking her for giving him back his faith seemed inadequate.

She squeezed his hand. "Bottom line? I don't trust Vince."

"And that's why you didn't share the information."

"Maddie Timmons is alive and she's counting on us to help her stay that way."

He was humbled by Avery's dedication to a woman she didn't know. "I'll trust your judgment on this."

She smiled. "Now that's progress."

Chapter Fourteen

"You may find this hard to believe, but I do have a business to run." Trevor didn't bother with sitting at his desk, because Russell wouldn't be staying long. If he harassed Sela again, he wouldn't even be allowed in the building. Good executive assistants were hard to find, and Sela Andrews was exceptional. Trevor wasn't about to waste his investment in training her simply because Russell couldn't control his temper.

"This is more important."

"I truly doubt that."

"I need some of your men." Russell dropped into the chair closest to Trevor's desk and crossed his ankle over his opposite knee.

Apparently Russell missed the fact he was the only one sitting. Also forgot he didn't have any say in Orion. "Excuse me?"

"The ones I sent to take care of Avery Walters failed."

Not exactly new information. He'd put a man on Luke right after Russell's earlier call. The status report refuting all of Russell's claims didn't surprise him. According to Trevor's man, nothing in Luke's demeanor or actions suggested he'd lost a member of his team. The comings and goings at his house had not changed. Holden hadn't moved out.

Most interesting was the men's ability to dodge a tail. Impressive as always. Wherever they kept going remained a mystery. They consistently went in and out, always leaving a male with the women, and switched their driving routes each time. Trevor seriously considered hacking the traffic cameras to track their movements. He would have done it if he didn't think Adam already had control of that computer system. Last thing Trevor wanted was for Luke and his agents to trace anything back to Orion or its offices.

Trevor guessed Recovery had set up a new shop. He'd find it, but he had other priorities at the moment. Namely, the irritating blowhard planted in his office.

"Are you sure?" Trevor asked.

"I have confirmation she's very much alive."

"I seem to remember you calling and bragging about having neutralized the Recovery problem," Trevor said with more than a little sarcasm.

"That may have been premature."

"May? That sounds like an understatement."

"Was."

It felt good to make Russell admit his failure. "Interesting."

"Caleb Mattern is alive, as well."

Trevor viewed that as a positive thing, but he didn't mention that. He leaned against his desk with his hands balanced behind him. "Your men really did fail, didn't they?"

"One is dead and the other will be when I get my hands on him."

They shared a significant loss of life where Recovery was concerned. Trevor lost more men than he could tolerate. "So, why are you here? You could have told me you were wrong without having to see me."

Russell's jaw clenched. "You train soldiers for this sort of work."

"I run a company, not the military." Not a formal militia anyway. Most of the troops Trevor had at his disposal were former military. Many had substantial training before signing up with him. All would fight to the death…for the right price.

"I'm not in the mood for word games or your pretend indifference."

"Why do I care what you want?"

Russell's hands curled into fists. "Because I'm in charge of this operation."

It amazed Trevor that Russell still thought so. "I see."

"I cannot afford to lose any more men."

The man could not be this simple. "You are not borrowing any of my employees."

"Avery Walker grabbed the email." Russell pushed up from the chair and started pacing. "Do you understand what I'm saying?"

"Apparently not."

"This is a disaster."

Trevor couldn't tell if this was a bit of unnecessary

Russell drama or if an integral piece of information was now public. If it was the latter there was only one person to blame. Russell. How hard was it to keep one email from getting out into the open?

"What's in it?" Trevor asked, wanting to be clear about what had Russell in a lather.

"I don't know. It's some sort of code."

Just as he suspected. Drama. "Then why are you worried?"

"Aren't you?"

ADAM'S FACE POPPED UP on the monitor in the middle of the console. Zach sat at the warehouse tech counter and tapped on the keyboard. Two seconds later Holden's face showed up on the left screen. Avery crowded between Luke and Caleb as they stood behind Zach.

Luke folded his arms behind his back. "We're all on conference. Go ahead."

"Have you started the tracking?" Adam asked.

Zach kept right on typing and a third monitor started racing with lines of computer script. "Yep."

She leaned closer to Caleb. "Did I miss something?"

"Zach is making sure no one is tapping into our communication."

"Could someone do that?"

Luke answered her. "Consider it a precaution."

"Before Adam starts, we need to have an agreement on a related issue," Caleb said.

She had no idea what he planned to say. She also wondered how he was standing. The fact he leaned hard enough on the back of Zach's chair to flip the chair over was a bad sign to her way of thinking. The man should be in bed. Be resting.

The way he hobbled around the room pretending he was fine was downright pathetic. She was all for letting a guy save his ego, but Caleb was jeopardizing his recovery. If she had to enlist Luke's help to get Caleb to sit down, she would. They had to get through this conference first.

"What's up?" Holden asked the question, but all of the men were focused on Caleb.

He glanced in her direction before speaking. "No one tells Vince about the email we grabbed pre-bomb or Maddie Timmons being alive."

Luke frowned. "Didn't you already do that?"

"No," Zach said as he leaned back in the chair and then quickly sat up again when Caleb bobbled behind him.

Luke took in the physical byplay and Caleb's questionable leg but didn't comment on it. Part of Avery wanted Luke to order Caleb to sit but deep down she knew that was the wrong way to handle the situation. The last thing he needed was his friends to focus on his injury instead of his strength. A man like Caleb needed to feel needed. She understood that now. How she'd missed it before she fired him she didn't know.

"Why the secrecy?" Luke asked.

"Avery doesn't trust him."

"Zach!" she sputtered. She'd never sputtered in her life, but these guys had her totally off her game. She was accustomed to being in control. She was in charge in her lab. At home there. She could…

Luke nodded. "Okay."

"What?" Her breath stopped in her chest. As she looked around at the men, she saw instant agreement with Luke's curt comment. "You all agree?"

"We can hold off if you want us to." Adam shuffled some papers on his desk as he talked.

The sudden show of trust almost knocked her backward. "Just because I said so?"

Luke shrugged. "I admit I'd like to know your reasoning, but it's not important. If you want us to keep quiet on this we will."

For the first time she looked at Caleb. He stood there, sweat gathering on his forehead as he struggled to stand up. Somewhere along the line she'd gone from the woman they all tolerated because Rod foisted her on them, to someone they listened to. She'd spent hours worrying about how by protecting her they couldn't be out watching over Maddie. None of that seemed to matter to them right now. They weren't talking to the woman who once hurt Caleb. They were accepting her as one of their own.

She wasn't a crier and didn't burst into tears just because, but feeling as if she belonged somewhere almost pushed her there. She was so shocked she explained her theory about Vince without any hesitation. It came out in one long-winded sentence.

After an extra second of silence, Adam jumped in. "Now let me fill you in."

It was that simple. They all turned to Adam as though what she said wasn't a big deal. Forget that they had a relationship with Vince. They sided with her instincts. The relief almost knocked her over.

"We all know Maddie is alive. I moved in next door and made contact," Adam said.

"What does that mean?" Avery whispered to Caleb.

He smiled back. "She's attractive and he's trying not to mention that fact."

Adam looked up from the papers in front of him and glared at Caleb. "Thanks to the files David Brennan provided, we also know all three women had the same WitSec handler for a short period of time."

"Russell Ambrose," Zach said.

Adam nodded. "Good guess."

"That's not necessarily significant since Rod's also tied to these women and we know he didn't kill two of them," Holden pointed out.

"But Rod doesn't have a pattern of communication with Bram Walters, a man we know was digging around in WitSec and keeping secret files. And I know Rod doesn't because I checked, so if anyone wants to get angry about that, do it and then get over it." Adam waited for a response, but when no one spoke up he continued. "Rod also doesn't have suspect deposits in a hidden checking account."

Caleb stopped shifting his weight around. "How much we talking?"

"Hundred grand."

Caleb whistled. "Damn."

"They're small deposits made into different accounts. It took a while to track it down, but after I accounted for his pay and some miscellaneous deposits, it was easy to see the pattern."

"Nice job," Luke said.

"That doesn't mean he's working alone." Adam adjusted his glasses. "I don't have any proof, but I doubt he is."

Caleb's hands tightened on Zach's chair as he spoke. "Russell strikes me as ruthless but not brilliant. I doubt he has the stones to make this work."

She had a few theories, but she wondered what everyone else was thinking. "Who do you think—"

Holden didn't let her finish. "Trevor Walters."

Luke shook his head. "Couldn't have anything to do with the fact you hate him?"

"True, but he's got the men with the expertise to pull off building sweeps and car bombs," Holden said.

She snorted. "I'm not impressed."

Zach turned around and stared at her. "Because?"

"You guys have beaten them all. If these guys are so well trained and there are so many of them, why haven't they made inroads into defeating you? As far as I can tell, the only side with casualties is theirs."

They didn't pound their collective chests in victory, but the room practically hummed with satisfaction. She didn't say it to win their favor. She truly believed it. They beat back everyone sent their way. They did it with a quiet dignity and strength. She admired them for it.

And she loved Caleb.

The thought floated through her mind and stayed there. She'd been half in love with him when he turned her away two years ago. Not having any finality to the relationship left her with an open wound. Seeing him again made it itch and burn. Realizing she'd hurt him, that the lack of trust once ran both ways, that she was equally responsible for where they were and how they got there, allowed her to heal.

Luke brought her attention back to the WitSec situation. "Sounds like it's time for me to meet with Trevor again."

Holden groaned. Caleb swore.

"Why?" she asked.

"If he sent men after you and Caleb, we might have the advantage by showing up with you very much alive. Trevor isn't one who flinches, but I'd like to make him try."

"Caleb is not going anywhere." She dropped that bombshell and waited for a response.

"Excuse me?" The deadly cold in Caleb's voice was hard to miss. Luke even stepped back a little.

"You can barely stand." She waved her hand at him because his crunched-up body position said more than she could. "We should load you up with painkillers and throw you in bed."

"He'll be sitting." Adam sounded amused.

She didn't find him funny right now. "You are not helping."

"Sorry," Adam mumbled, even though he didn't look at all contrite.

"And what do you mean by sitting?" she asked.

"I'll set the time and place," Luke said. "We'll control the access."

"I still say no."

Caleb ground his teeth together. "Not your call."

She refused to back down. "It should be."

Caleb matched her anger with some of his own. "And I don't know why Luke thinks you're coming along."

"Of course I am."

Luke cleared his throat. "I need to see if I can shake Trevor up, Avery. Seeing Caleb might do it. And you're coming along because if Trevor's involved, he needs to know there's someone out here who can make life very tough for him."

"You're making her a target," Caleb shouted, and the room grew silent.

She wasn't about to jeopardize Luke's plans. The idea scared the heck out of her, but she knew these men would keep her safe. She also knew she couldn't sit back and wait for another witness to die. "I'm fine with that."

Caleb glared at Luke over the top of her head. "I'm not."

Luke didn't look away. "I don't love it either, but we can contain it."

"I'm assuming I'll take over from there," Adam said.

"Exactly. Adam will be ready. His job is to see if Trevor reaches out to Russell or anyone else."

She had to talk some sense into them, at least about Caleb. Doing it in a group wasn't working. She'd take Luke aside and convince him. There was no way he could get into a car, go somewhere and act with his usual superspy perfection.

In the meantime, she'd do what she could to put

Caleb's mind at ease about her participation. "And you can do that from West Virginia?"

Adam winked at her. "I can do it from anywhere."

Chapter Fifteen

Twenty-four hours later Caleb still hadn't cooled off. He sat in a private room of a near-empty restaurant right off Capitol Hill. Luke set up the meeting and gave Trevor almost no time to get there. It was the best way to ensure he couldn't bug the place or set his own plan into motion.

"Is he going to show?" Avery asked as she played with the silverware.

Luke leaned against the door frame and stared out into the main dining room. "Definitely."

"Are you going to talk to me again or just keep pretending I'm not here?" she asked Caleb.

He didn't have the control he needed to respond. Not yet. Not after she spent the night all over him, guiding him into her and exhausting him so that he couldn't do anything but pass out in a deep sleep. Then she tried to leave him at home this morning. Actually crushed a painkiller into his coffee and tried to drug him. So much for a pleasant morning-after. And good thing he liked to watch her and was remembering how good she felt the night before while he glanced at her long fingers, or he might have missed her attempted drugging.

"Caleb?"

He held up a hand to her. "No."

"I was doing it for you."

Part of him knew that. The rational part, the same part he was ignoring at the moment. "I'm a grown man."

She clanged the silverware loud enough to be heard on the next block. "And I want you to be safe."

"I outweigh you by sixty pounds." He was also taller, louder and meaner, but he left those details out.

Her mouth twisted as if she tasted something sour. "That really doesn't matter since you can't walk."

"You don't have to bring that up every minute."

"I do if you insist on acting like you're fine."

Luke glanced at him over his shoulder. "I thought her plan was pretty ingenuous. Seemed like something Claire would try. Drugging is her style."

Avery wore a huge smile. "Thank you."

"That's not a compliment," Caleb mumbled.

"It sort of is since I married the lady." Luke came away from the wall and slid into the booth on the other side of Avery. The good-hearted tone had vanished. "He's here."

Avery shifted in her seat as she tried to see outside the small room. "Alone?"

"Trevor is not the entourage type."

"Good morning." Trevor appeared at the opening, wearing his expensive suit and usual smirk. He waved off the waiter and eyed up his table companions.

Caleb wanted to stand up and take a swing at the guy. He didn't think he could manage the former without help, and Luke had specifically forbidden the latter.

"Caleb, Luke. Good to see you both again, and under better circumstances this time."

"Your brother did have quite a showing at his funeral," Luke said.

Caleb nodded. "Thanks to us."

Trevor's attention turned to Avery. "And you are?"

"Avery Walker." Caleb answered for her. Also nudged her thigh to get her to stop rattling the spoon and fork in her hand.

"Well, this is a pleasure." Trevor slid into the U-shaped booth but stayed at the very end.

"If you say so," Caleb said.

"Answer me this, Luke. Exactly how many guns are pointed at me at this particular moment?" Trevor folded and unfolded the napkin in front of him.

"Two under the table and one from a discreet distance."

He turned to Avery. "Did you realize the men you're with are so bloodthirsty?"

"I wanted a gun of my own but they said no."

When Trevor's smug smile faded, Caleb wanted to hug Avery for her bravado. She didn't back down or panic. She recognized Trevor's test and passed it.

"We thought you'd like to see Avery and Caleb for yourself." Luke motioned to them.

Trevor frowned and managed to look sincere in his confusion. "I'm afraid I don't understand."

"They are alive."

Trevor nodded. "I can see that."

Caleb tightened his hold on his gun. It rested on his good knee and he was itching to shoot. "The plan didn't work."

"Ah, I see what's happening here." Trevor glanced around the table. "Caleb has gotten into some sort of trouble and you immediately assume I am the cause."

The man acted so innocent, yet guilt dripped off him. Other people looked at him and saw a charitable businessman. Caleb saw a lowlife dressed in a big-boy suit. "Something like that."

"I assure you I have no problem with Recovery or its agents. I certainly don't have an issue with Ms. Walker." Trevor bowed in his seat as he said it.

Luke shifted in his seat. "We had a deal, Trevor."

Trevor did some shifting of his own. He probably thought he was about to be shot. Caleb liked the idea of Trevor losing control.

"I have honored our agreement," Trevor said.

"My information says otherwise."

"Then you are being lied to, Luke."

Caleb's patience was about to expire. He wanted to be home, anywhere but there, and for this mess to be over. "Your brother was involved in WitSec and now you are."

"I'm a businessman. Nothing more."

"I told you what I would do if I found out you were messing with Recovery." The dead calm to Luke's voice made Avery jump.

Trevor didn't seem to notice the change in tone from neutral to furious. "I can only assume I'm being implicated by someone who wishes to cause trouble. I can assure you—"

"Russell Ambrose." They were the first words Avery had spoken, but they had an impact.

Trevor flinched. "Excuse me?"

"You know him. Don't pretend otherwise," Caleb said.

Trevor sighed. "Unfortunately, that's true."

"You don't like him." Avery phrased it as a statement instead of a question.

"Not particularly."

"Why?" she asked.

"I find him...weak."

As far as Caleb was concerned, that was the least offensive of Russell's qualities. "We believe he's corrupt."

Trevor shrugged. "Wouldn't surprise me."

There it was. The subtle turn in the conversation from verbal maneuvering to information gathering. Trevor had been biding his time, seeing what they knew. Caleb could tell because he and Luke had been doing the same thing. Give away little and try to take much. That was the theory for this sort of meeting.

"Anything you wish to share?" Luke asked right on cue.

Trevor rubbed a stiff crease into the middle of the cloth napkin. "Only that I hear he's come into money recently."

Luke nodded. "I hear that, too."

Caleb could feel the stillness fall over Avery as she held her breath. Caleb felt the rising tension, too. It was as if all the oxygen got sucked out of this part of the restaurant.

"Then we know the same information," Trevor said.

"I have to wonder if anyone else has come into money."

"I couldn't say."

Caleb expected some hesitation, but Trevor dove right in. Didn't pretend confusion or get up and leave. This was a man who wanted to deal.

"Anything you can say?" Luke asked.

"That if someone else is involved in this scheme, assuming there is one, the only way to get him is to lure him out into the open and catch him." Trevor's gaze traveled to Avery and stayed there. "Maybe there's something he wants. A job he hasn't finished."

It took all of Caleb's control to sit there and not react. As suspected, Russell wanted Avery out of the way.

"I'd hate to do something and then find out Russell had an army standing behind him." Luke stopped circling and went right for the deathblow.

"I can't speak to his connections, but I can say my men wouldn't do anything to protect him."

Luke's eyes narrowed. "Even if they were standing right there."

"Even then." Trevor smiled.

THE CONVERSATION WOUND down right after. When Trevor got up to leave, none of them stood. That was a sign of respect none of them felt he deserved.

Avery broke the silence as Trevor pushed open the

door and hit the street. "I don't even understand what just happened."

Caleb knew and tried to figure out a way to keep it from Avery, but she was a smart woman. If she thought about the conversation, she'd realize the truth. Reason it out and then volunteer to put her body right in the middle of danger.

"Trevor wants us to use you as a decoy. He'll make Russell think he has Orion's backing and then will pull his support." There, he'd said it. Now he'd spend every ounce of energy talking her out of helping.

"He wants to set up Russell," Luke added.

She ignored the part where her life was in danger. She took the news as if it was the weather report. "So, Trevor is guilty?"

Luke shrugged. "Of a lot of things, I imagine."

"I still—"

"He wants Russell gone and wants it done before anything happens to you or Maddie," Luke said.

Avery looked at both men before saying anything. "You got all of that from the cryptic conversation?"

Caleb knew it was time to step in and stop this nonsense. Avery was not going to get into the middle of this battle. She was far too involved already. Much more and he'd never sleep again.

"Yes, but it doesn't matter what Trevor wants or suggests," Caleb said, letting her hear the determination in his voice.

"Why?"

"Because you are not going anywhere near Russell."

Chapter Sixteen

Russell stood at the steps of the Lincoln Memorial. "Why the change?"

It was sunny and bright, the kind of day residents love because the humidity hadn't rolled in and snow was long gone. Tourists walked around them, taking group pictures and staring in reverent silence at the statue behind the regal columns.

Trevor didn't notice any of it. He was too busy laying his trap. It was time for Russell to be terminated and if Trevor could get Recovery to do most of the work, then all the better.

"Because you are correct," he said. "Parts of this scheme can be traced back to me. That means inaction is not an option."

"I can lay all of it on your doorstep if I choose. Don't forget that."

Trevor motioned for them to go down the steps and walk along the reflecting pool. "Understood."

He had narrowed down the hiding place for the tape to three locations. Every inch of Russell's home and office had been searched without success. Mail had been traced. Post office boxes had been checked. That left a box in his sister's name, the briefcase he always carried and somewhere Trevor hadn't discovered yet.

His money was on the briefcase. It made sense. Russell never took a hand off it. Everywhere he went, it went. Something important was in that briefcase. Something he didn't want out of his sight. Sure, he could have handed it off to someone, but Russell didn't have close friends and his sister's house had been searched.

"I am not willing to lose everything I have over three women in witness protection." Which wasn't exactly a lie. Trevor didn't want to lose everything over anyone, whether that be his ex-wife, Russell or even his dead brother.

"They aren't worth your concern. Trust me. I have access to their files and know what they did. If the public knew they financially supported these types of criminals, the outcry would be deafening."

Trevor noticed Russell didn't think of his victims as human. He'd demoted them in his mind to subhuman. "Which is why you were willing to take the money to kill them."

"I didn't kill anyone."

The man could not be this simple or have this little understanding about consequences. "Because you didn't pull the trigger?"

Russell stopped at the edge of the water. "What is this plan you have?"

"Avery Walker in her lab."

He shook his head. "I tried that already. By now the

security has been fixed and neither Avery nor anyone else can get in without new codes."

"Your failed attempt was not with my men."

"You missed my other point. Gaining an entrance."

"I can handle that part."

Russell looked up and down the mall. "What makes you so sure she'll go back there or that she can get in?"

"She was working on something when she left the lab. If we want her to come back, we make it easier for her to return." When Russell continued to stare with a look that could be described only as simple, Trevor gave more clues. "I'll have her boss let her know about the break-in."

"I don't get it."

Trevor hid a sigh. "Right now Avery likely believes she can't go back into the lab. She's probably worried she'll be arrested or at the very least detained since the last time she was there people died."

"I think she's right."

"If she gets a message that explains what happened while she was on vacation and makes it so she's in the clear, she'll feel emboldened to go back in."

"And?"

"You will be there."

Russell was even slower than usual today. "You mean your men."

"They will back you up, but the real dirty work is yours this time, Russell. If you want to take her, do it. My guys will help you get in and take her out. They won't, however, do your killing for you."

Russell stepped closer. His back teeth were slammed together so that his words came out strained. "I'm not a killer."

"And I'm not paying someone to do it for you."

That fast, Russell's anger dissipated. "That's not much of an offer."

"It's access and backup. That's all you're going to get from me."

"You still forget who is in charge."

Trevor was quite aware who ran this show and it wasn't Russell. "And you forget which one of us has clout. Take the deal. It's the best one you're going to get."

LUKE STEPPED UP TO THE conference table and stood across from Caleb and Avery. They were the only three left in the building. They had eaten and fought and now sat in silence from the post-Trevor meeting. No one moved. Neither conceded a point or backed down.

"I just got the call from Trevor. Everything is in place," Luke said.

Caleb didn't lift his head. He continued to trace a pattern only he could see on the tabletop in front of him. "I don't care. The answer is still no."

Avery had heard every argument. Ever since those failed, Caleb turned to simple orders. In his mind, she was not going to do it and that was that.

She disagreed. "I'm going to the lab as planned."

When he lifted his head, his eyes burned with fury. "You are not sacrificing your life for this assignment. Hell, it's not even an assignment. We're working blind, following things we think are leads. We've been looking for any sign anywhere of Rod and have come up empty. Adam is the best at what he does and he can't find a trace of Rod. The whole thing is nuts."

She reached out to put her hand over his, but he pulled back before she could touch him. "Caleb—"

He stood up so fast, he almost fell. He grabbed for the chair next to him and steadied his muscles. "Consider yourself grounded."

"No."

"Luke, a little help here?" Caleb turned to his friend. "You've locked Claire in the house. Whether you want to admit it or not, you know exactly how I feel."

Luke shrugged. "That's a little different."

"How?"

"I'm married to Claire. I love her."

The words echoed throughout the two-story space. If Luke wanted to bring the conversation to a halt, he'd found the perfect way. Also ripped her heart out in the process.

The reminder that Claire meant everything to him was a harsh reality at the moment. Avery wanted that. Yes, Caleb was fighting her on playing the role of decoy. It was in his nature to be protective. It even went further than that. He cared.

But he heard the word *love* and his face closed up.

He stormed out of the room, cheeks puffing and rushing as fast as his injured leg would allow. He grumbled and swore and generally looked ready to fall over at any minute.

Luke waited until Caleb went into the bathroom and

slammed the door behind him. "That was an interesting reaction."

"You wanted to antagonize him?" She couldn't hide the shock in her voice.

Luke ignored her question. "You know, I actually agree with him about the assignment."

"I know."

"My preference is to leave you both here."

"Not possible."

Luke stared at the space from where Caleb had just disappeared. "Maybe we could—"

"Russell is going to keep coming. He's trying to protect his butt. He can't let me live. And when he's done with me, he'll go after Maddie." Avery knew Luke understood all of this. He was searching for another way and, like her, not finding it.

It wasn't as if she had a death wish. She didn't. But she had to see this through, for her, for Damon, even for Rod.

"Adam is ready on Maddie's end. If there's a problem there, he'll step in," Luke explained.

Avery knew the WitSec part of the problem could end with Adam taking a bullet or being too late to save Maddie. He wasn't living with the woman. He couldn't be there every second. And those scenarios didn't even cover all the other problems like the corruption in high places and Rod's unexplained disappearance.

No, there was nothing controlled about this situation. Avery appreciated that Luke professed to have that much faith in his men, but she could see the worry in his eyes.

"And what about the next WitSec participant? If Russell gets away with it now, he'll do it again. The money is a big lure and Adam says Russell needs it. I'm not sure what he's spending it all on, but he's running through it."

"Adam thinks it's gambling."

The time for arguing was over. She'd heard from Caleb all the awful stories of what could happen to her if she got trapped or taken or shot. She was resigned to move forward, terror and all. "I have to do this."

Luke stared at her for what felt like thirty minutes but probably didn't amount to more than a few seconds. "Before we go tomorrow, you might want to take a minute and tell Caleb what you need to tell him."

The man was too perceptive. "What does that mean?"

"We both know the story isn't as simple as you firing him to protect your job."

This was part of their acceptance. The group now recognized her history with Caleb as being more than a one-sided tale of a nasty ex-girlfriend. Only Caleb still believed the worst. Oh, he'd convinced himself it was okay now. He never said it, but she could see it written on his face. He'd decided to forgive her. He didn't even understand that he should ask for forgiveness, as well.

"Maybe he needs to believe that I'm the bad guy here," she suggested, wondering if that was true.

"Or maybe he deserves the truth."

FIFTEEN MINUTES LATER she sat on the edge of the bed and waited for Caleb to limp into the room. She was going to try one more time to explain her side, to make him listen.

"Why did you fire me?" he asked as he moved to stand in front of her.

He couldn't have surprised her more if he'd started to sing opera tunes. He'd avoided this topic and everything that passed between them for two years. Now he hit it head-on, throwing off her well-laid plans to tackle the issue.

"Honestly?"

"I'm not sure why I'd want you to be dishonest about this."

She had to bend her neck back to look up at him. "You didn't belong there."

"That doesn't make sense."

She gave him the party line, the same line she'd been saying over and over as he ignored her. "You broke protocol and threatened cases."

"I never—"

She held up her hand to stop the flow of defensive words. "There was nothing wrong with your skills or your knowledge. You were meant for more than testing in a lab."

"You still expect me to believe you fired me to *help* me."

She hadn't looked at it that way when it happened. She was hoping to scare him straight and get him back in a lab. Then he ran from her, emotionally and physically, and she scrambled.

"Yes."

He dropped down next to her on the mattress and

stretched his injured leg out in front of him. "I don't buy it. But you know what? It doesn't matter. I'm done living in the past."

The words sliced through her. They cut into her flesh and went right down to her vital organs. "So, when this is over, I'm out and you're moving on?"

His eyes widened. "Did I say that?"

"I don't know what you're saying."

He took her hand in both of his. "I forgive you."

The warm touch of his skin contrasted with the words that filled her brain with a wild fury. "For what?"

"The firing. For picking your job over me. For not fighting for me with the higher-ups. All of it. It's over and we need to put it behind us." He kissed the back of her hand.

She wanted to strangle him. "You're letting me off the hook?"

"I'm trying to be a grown-up. Forgive and forget."

She was sure that in his mind this all made sense. He acted as if he had made some huge sacrifice by giving up his hatred for her.

"But you don't forget," she said, knowing she was right about this and being sure it was the one thing that would destroy them.

"You're not listening."

She slipped her hand out of his and stood up. "What about my apology?"

This time he was the one who had to look up. "What?"

"You resented the fact I got a promotion."

"That's not true. You were there longer, had more experience. You deserved it." He rubbed his injured knee.

She tried not to care. Forced her legs not to bend, not to let her body slip back to the floor and massage it for him. "Then why did you try to sabotage me?"

"What are you talking about?"

The shock was evident in his voice, but she didn't back down. Having him forgive her would have been good enough right after they broke up. She would have taken on all the responsibility and tried to work it out.

But she deserved more. She was worth more. And she secretly knew he would never let it go if he didn't understand the whole truth.

"You sit there and talk about everything I did wrong. Want to know your list?" She'd held it in for so long that the words flowed now without any help from her brain. "You came to me when you were still raw and bitter about your marriage. She'd made you leave the navy. She made you take a job at the lab. She left you after you changed your entire life, and you were ticked off."

He struggled to stand up. His bad leg kept sliding under him as he struggled to get traction. He finally gave up and slumped back on the mattress. "That didn't have anything to do with what happened with us."

"Of course it did. You were mad at her and closed yourself off from me. The sex was great, but you held back from giving me anything else. When I specifically asked you not to go beyond the job anymore, not to put me in the position where I had to discipline you, you agreed. And then you did it anyway."

His eyes widened. "Avery, I never—"

"You talk about me picking the job over you. You are the one who picked your side work, the exact work you were not permitted to do and promised you would stop, over me. You put me in that untenable position, in a situation I couldn't win. When I did what I had to do and fired you, you went insane. Called me names, walked away."

"I was blindsided."

"No, Caleb. You weren't. You were angry that once again a woman was dictating what happened with your career."

This time he wrestled his way to his feet. He put his hands on her upper arms and leaned against her. "You've got this backward."

"Once you were out, I knew I had to help. You see, I was dumb enough to fall for you. Really fall. For me it wasn't about sex. It was about building something with you. So, I pulled every string to help you get the job I knew you should have. One with Rod."

"I didn't know." Caleb shook his head as his cheeks sunk.

"Because you wouldn't listen. When I tried to talk to you, you turned away."

He rubbed a hand through his hair. "I thought—"

"I'd picked the job over you. Yeah, I know." She heard the accusations in her sleep. "I kept hoping you'd settle down and come back, but it never happened. I even swallowed my pride and begged you to come back. Do you know what that did to me?"

"I can...no..."

"In the end, I had to come for you one more time."

He lifted his arms and then let them drop to his sides again. "I don't know what to say."

"I don't want you to say anything." That wasn't true. She wanted him to wipe the stunned look off his face and apologize. She was desperate for him to get it. For him to wake up and see her standing there waiting for him.

But he just stood there, mouth half open and confusion etched on every line of his face.

"Want to know the sad thing, Caleb?" When he didn't say anything, she took the plunge. "I loved you then."

"Avery."

"And I love you now."

His hand shook as he reached for her again. "We need to talk about this."

She knew he wouldn't say it back, but that didn't make the slight any easier. The loss ripped her wide open. She waited for her heart to fall out and flop around on the floor. "We can't."

"Why?"

"This time you didn't see me drug your drink." She glanced at the clock. "You should be asleep any minute."

And by the time he woke up, she'd be on her assignment.

His eyes drooped, as if saying the words sucked all the energy right out of him. "You're running?"

"I learned it from you."

Chapter Seventeen

Russell stood in the back parking lot at the lab and looked at his bodyguard, Howard. The man towered over six feet. His shoulders almost touched both sides of the doorway. He had guns and knives hidden in his clothes and on his body.

Howard was new and dedicated.

He was insurance.

Trevor promised to provide backup. He had three men going to the lab with Russell. They were meeting in an hour, just before four. All three had tactical training and a list of other honors that Trevor provided but Russell ignored. They would follow his orders and not flinch when Russell took care of Avery.

Trevor made all of the promises. He'd gone from sarcastic to helpful, and Russell didn't trust the change. Maybe Trevor was being truthful and he finally realized the looming danger to his reputation.

Or maybe this was a setup.

Trevor had always underestimated him. The man thought he was so smart, so in control. If that were true, he wouldn't be dancing around as Russell ordered.

As if Russell would enter a dangerous situation without having one of his own men there, waiting, ready to pounce if needed. Things could go wrong. Alliances could get confused.

Howard would take care of all those possibilities. He knew the target. He also knew he could be fighting attacks from every direction, including one from the Recovery agents. Russell wasn't taking any chances this time. He was going in and finding out what Avery knew. Howard could handle Caleb or whatever man Luke sent his way.

Avery was all his.

CALEB TRIED TO SHAKE the lethargy from his muscles. He felt something hard under his head and the usual ache in his leg. He started to think the unrelenting pain was normal, as if it would never leave him. Still, he had to ease up on the painkillers.

Then his mind clicked and he sat up straight, banging his head off the shelf above him.

Zach chuckled. "'Bout time you woke up."

"Where are we?" Caleb took in the computer equipment and blackened van windows.

"Surveillance van outside of the lab."

"What?"

"She knocked you on your a—"

He crowded in on Zach and ignored the scream of pain from his knee to his groin. "Where is Avery?"

"There." Zach pointed at the monitor above his head.

"I'm stopping this right now." Caleb tried to stand

up and fell back down. In the cramped quarters it was even harder for him to maneuver. Shuffling his feet only highlighted the pain. Having to fight off the cloudy feeling in his brain didn't help either.

"Whoa." Zach reached out and helped Caleb back onto the small bench behind the computer chair. "You go in now and you'll make a mess. Probably get her hurt, or worse. Just let this play out. It's under control."

"She's being set up. Anything can happen." Fury burned through him all over again. The idea of her being in danger filled him with darkness.

Ever since she'd come back into his life, the deep mistrust had evaporated. And when she explained about her view of their breakup, his heart ripped in two. She had tried to tell him, to win him back. When that didn't work, she tried to make his life better. Still, he pushed her away and judged.

He had no excuse. He'd been in a bad marriage and tried to keep from heading down that road again. But Avery wasn't his wife and she'd deserved better.

And she loved him.

The knowledge cleared out every nasty thought and made everything possible again. With those simple words, that incredible admission, she handed him back his life. But he could lose her before he ever got the chance to let her know he understood, to beg her to give him another chance and forgive his stupidity. The thought made his stomach flip. It was too awful to contemplate.

After everything they'd been through, they deserved another shot. Not because he'd forgiven her or any of the ridiculous things he'd been saying in his head. He wanted a chance because he loved her.

The realization wasn't gentle or happy. It snuck up and banged him over the head. Now that he recognized the feeling, he wondered if it had always hovered in his heart. He'd shut her out for so long, but it was impossible to do so any longer. Dread and happiness mixed together until he didn't know what to feel or do.

"This is why they wanted to leave you at home," Zach said.

"What?"

"I snuck you in the van."

"Avery thinks I'm at the warehouse?" That meant she didn't even know he was here for her.

"Luke ordered that you remain there."

"For God's sake, why?"

"He thought you were too emotionally attached to this one to have perspective." Different images of the lab flipped by on the screens in front of Zach.

"You disagreed."

"Seems to me a man should be able to watch over his woman."

Caleb couldn't see Zach's face, but he could hear the smile in Zach's voice. Caleb couldn't muster any jokes. He was too busy drowning in worry and guilt.

Man, he wanted Avery to be his. Forever. He hoped and prayed he hadn't blown it so far apart that he couldn't put it back together again.

"I'm not sure that's what she is," he said.

"Then you're not as smart as I thought you were."

He had to snap out of it. To fight off the mix of

pain drugs and confusion. She needed him. Even if he couldn't rush in and help, he could make sure the intel she got was right. He could run behind the scenes so that when she walked out of the building healthy and whole, he could grab her and tell her all those words she deserved to hear.

He took the seat next to Zach. "Tell me what's happening."

"Russell is right here, just inside the front door. That's one of Trevor's men with him. The other two are waiting just outside the building."

"Avery?"

The image on the monitor switched. "Right here. Holden is in the walk-in freezer. Luke is watching over her."

Caleb almost touched the screen. Despite the grainy image, he saw her beautiful face. For the first time in a long time he felt hope, the kind of happiness that came when a man saw a future and the woman he wanted in it.

"Put the images up side by side. Use the third screen to flip through the other rooms just to be safe."

Zach smiled. "Done."

"She's going to be okay."

"Good to have you back."

Russell and his guard headed for the lab. "They're moving in."

Caleb watched the third monitor, the one with the rotating screens. "Go back."

"What?"

"Number three. There." Caleb pointed at the monitor. "Who is that?"

A big guy with a gun. He'd broken off from the others. He put the body count in the building at one too many.

Zach shook his head. "Don't know but not a worker. He's moving like paid help."

"Like a mercenary."

Zach typed something into his watch. "Don't panic. I'll get word to Luke."

Caleb had moved past panic. His nerve endings were screaming for him to do something and do it fast. "How many men did Trevor send?"

"Three."

"Then Russell brought this one." Caleb struggled to his feet. His knee wouldn't cooperate. Wouldn't bend.

Zach stood up at the same time. "I'll go."

"You man this."

"Caleb, you can barely move."

"I'm not letting my woman face this without me."

Chapter Eighteen

Avery's mind kept wandering back to the scene last night, and she kept forcing it to the task at hand. While Luke watched, she performed a fake experiment. It was all for show. The idea was to lure Russell in, get him to think she was on to something. Something that she'd be willing to come out in public to do.

"You're doing great," Luke whispered.

"What if they don't come?"

"They're here."

The news froze her bones. For a second she couldn't move or breathe. She'd survived one shoot-out in this lab. Now she had to face another.

"It's going to be okay."

"I know." She didn't. She absolutely didn't.

Luke stepped back and knocked on the metal door to the refrigerator compartment. It opened a fraction. Holden didn't pop out, but she knew he was there.

"Almost time?" she asked.

Luke looked over her shoulder. "In a minute, you're going to turn around and head into the fridge. Holden and I will take it from here."

"Russell isn't stupid. He can tell the difference between a man and a woman," she said.

"Russell will see a white coat and it won't register for a second. That's all we need." Luke glanced at his watch. "Here he comes."

She didn't look. If it turned out Trevor had figured out a clever way to wipe them all out…no, she couldn't let herself entertain that possibility. It was too awful. The only good thing about that scenario was that Caleb would be safe. He was at the warehouse. He didn't have to face down gunfire.

As she turned, she heard the gunman enter the room. He was faster than she expected. She just reached the door when Russell walked in. She looked into Holden's hiding place but didn't go in. She turned around to face Russell instead.

Luke swore under his breath. "Avery."

"Do not move." Russell moved into the room with his guards behind him.

The three looked like a wall of evil to Avery. She saw all that hate and regretted every minute of the past few hours. She shouldn't have confronted Caleb. She should have let it go and not pushed. She'd see the shock and sadness in his eyes until the day she died.

But at least she'd told him she loved him. She hoped on some level that mattered to him. That he'd find some comfort in it instead of being terrified of loving again.

Luke raised his weapon as he pulled her behind him. "Stay back."

Russell shook his head. Made an annoying tsk-tsk

sound as he did it. "It's three against one. Lower the gun."

"No."

"Then we'll shoot it out of your hands."

Avery stepped forward even as Luke pulled her back. "Who are you?"

Russell pointed at her. "Ms. Walker, you have caused me a great deal of trouble."

The fact this vile creature knew her name made the contents of her stomach bubble. "Because I uncovered your murders."

"It's time for us to go." He wiggled his fingers at her.

Could he actually be so stupid as to think she'd go with him? "No."

"She's not going anywhere with you." Luke's harsh voice suggested he was willing to die for her.

In that moment she knew he would. She also knew she'd do anything, even if it meant leaving the room with Russell, to save Luke. To save any of them. But that shouldn't be necessary. The men by his side were working against Russell, he just didn't know it. That was the reason for the false confidence.

"Shoot him in the knee." Russell gave the order then turned around, heading back out toward the lobby.

"I wouldn't do that if I were you." Holden stepped out and called for her. "Avery, come here."

Russell spun around. "Any more of you in there?"

"I only need one gun to take you down," Luke said.

"If you move, Ms. Walker, I will have my men put a

hole in one of your protectors. Just how long will it be before I hit someone you care about?"

She took a deep breath. She knew the plan. This was okay. None of it was real except Russell's belief that he had won. "Fine."

Russell gave a nod of satisfaction. "Gentlemen. Guns on the floor."

Luke shook his head. "No."

Russell gave his men a hand signal but nothing happened. When he did it again, one of the guards actually lowered his weapon instead of aiming. A shot went through his back a second later. Blood spurted as his eyes went wide in shock.

Avery screamed before the poor man hit the ground.

Luke and Holden scrambled, trying to put something between them and the gunfire. When another man with Russell fell, sending a weapon spinning across the floor, the additional screams of horror caught in her throat. Her body went cold as the room exploded in action around her.

The remaining man tried to shoot Russell. Holden began firing. Luke tugged her closer, trying to tuck her between him and the workbench. Russell pulled back into the hall with a smile plastered on his face. His enjoyment registered with Avery right as a fourth man slipped into the room.

It happened in a flash. One second everyone was running for cover and firing. The next this man shot around her in Holden's direction then grabbed her arm and dragged her to Russell's side of the room.

When the gunfire stopped, Trevor's three men were

on the floor, ambushed by one of Russell's. She felt a man's beefy hand on her neck and the muzzle of his gun against her temple. Luke and Holden faced her, weapons up. There was blood on Luke's face and Holden had blood coming from a shot to the arm. Their clothes were torn and faces white, but she slumped in relief that neither looked seriously injured.

Only Russell came out clean. She decided that's what happened when a man hid from the fight and slinked out after.

Russell shook his head. "I had hoped to resolve this in an amicable fashion."

"Let her go," Luke said.

Holden nodded. "There are two of us. Whatever your guy does, Russell, you still get shot."

"But I have her." Russell tugged on her hair to prove his point.

The sharp pain in her scalp was nothing compared with the aches and pains everywhere else. The man with the hold around her head was pressing bruises into her skin. Not that she showed fear. She knew if Luke and Holden saw her in pain they might play it safe, and that could get them killed.

She wanted them in attack mode.

She wanted Caleb.

CALEB TRIED TO BE AS quiet as possible. His one leg dragged behind him. No matter how soft he tread, his steps made a soft rustling sound. He hoped the whirl of the fans would hide some of the sound. He also had the benefit of being behind the crowd.

Russell and his three Trevor-provided guards turned down the hall toward the labs. The stray held back. Caleb assumed it was his job to go in last and clean up anyone still standing. Since Trevor's men weren't supposed to harm anyone, they were looking at a potential surprise bloodbath here.

Caleb had to focus on the men. He couldn't think about Avery. If he did, he'd lose it.

He kept his back to the wall and slid his way along, letting friction hold him up and momentum keep him marching. He'd just turned the corner, putting the extra man in his sights, when the guy shifted and the shooting started.

Caleb's mind shouted at him to run. He had to get to Avery. Had to throw his body over hers. Protect her. She could not die. He could not lose her.

Fueled by nothing more than adrenaline and grit, he picked up his pace. Every step sent bolts of pain radiating through his body. He slammed his back teeth together to keep from shouting in pain. As he neared the doorway, he let his feet slide. A man went down right next to him a second later. His feet fell into the hall and his gun clattered against the tile floor.

Caleb forced his gaze away when he heard Avery screaming and Holden shouting. Caleb swore he heard someone laughing, as if this insane scene was anything but a horror. When the noise stopped, the acrid smell of smoke and fired ammunition filled the air. One of the men on the floor groaned. Then he heard the words he dreaded. They stopped him cold.

But I have her.

Leg or not, strength or not, he was going into that room and taking Russell out. No one was going to touch Avery. Caleb didn't care what he had to do or if he lost his life in the process.

Balancing against the wall, he inched closer to the door. Russell was making threats and ignoring Luke's orders to let Avery go. The raised voices provided the cover Caleb needed to slip in. He could get behind them, maybe get the jump on the guy who had Avery. Caleb couldn't see the man, but he knew from the conversation she was trapped.

He hoped Luke and Holden wouldn't shoot first and identify later as Caleb started counting down to his move. When he hit three, he plunged into the doorway, fighting to keep upright. Holden's stare connected with Caleb's right as he swung the weapon around.

Caleb used all his energy to shove Russell in the back. Caught off guard, the man stumbled forward into Luke. The commotion gave Caleb the opportunity he needed. He fired one shot into the back of the remaining attacker's head while Holden pulled Avery free. The big man dropped to the floor in a heap.

The last bit of strength in Caleb's leg gave out and he followed the other man down.

Russell wailed in fury. He grabbed for Avery but Luke held him back. Caleb saw Avery struggling to get to him and heard all the voices around him. He had just vowed to stand up, somehow, even if it meant crawling up the workbench, when Russell started shouting.

"This isn't over. Powerful people are involved. This will never get to trial."

Luke shook Russell by the collar. "Shut up."

"You think it stops with me? You have no idea."

"Who else?" Holden shouted.

"People with power and money. Ask Trevor…" Russell's comment gurgled to a stop.

The gunshot shook them all. They turned to the location of the shooter. One of Trevor's men rested against his gun. Blood seeped from the side of his neck, but he got off the shot.

Somehow, some way, Trevor had managed to silence them all.

Caleb couldn't summon up the energy to care. Other things mattered now. The most important was the woman standing not five feet away from him.

"Avery?"

She pulled free of Holden's grasp and ran to Caleb. Kneeling on the floor in front of him, half holding him up and weeping all the time, she covered his face in kisses as she professed her undying love. She didn't stop until she fit her mouth over his and stole the last of his breath with a head-spinning kiss that had Luke laughing.

Caleb had so much he wanted to say to her. "Avery—"

"I was wrong." She shook her head as she pressed her palms against his cheeks. "I blamed you for everything, but I did fire you. That was me. My insecurities about losing the job I wanted so badly."

After everything, she was still willing to take the blame and let him escape responsibility. It humbled him that she loved him that much, but it was wrong. "Don't say that."

"I should have talked to you."

He kissed her, trying to get her to understand that it was him not her who broke them apart. "You tried."

"Not hard enough."

"I wasn't ready to listen." In reality, he just wasn't ready for her. He was still too raw and bitter from his divorce to appreciate Avery or give her what she needed, but that was over.

He had her now and would never let her go.

"I could have—"

He just went with what was in his heart. "I love you."

She pulled back and stared at him with eyes filled with tears. "What?"

"I love you."

She shook her head. No words came out.

His heart broke a little right then. "What have I done to you that I tell you and you still don't believe?"

"What are you saying?"

He rested his forehead against hers. "I love you. Can't-see-straight kind of love you."

"About time." Luke didn't even try to whisper his comment.

Caleb ignored his friend and concentrated on the woman who meant everything to him. "You gave me this."

"This?" She sounded appalled.

"Recovery." He gestured toward Holden and Luke. "These two idiots and the rest of them. A life and a purpose."

She looked around at the bodies piled on the floor. "This is a disaster. You can't blame this on me."

Caleb put a hand under her chin and brought her face back to his. "I love you."

Her shoulders fell and her bruised face lit with a smile. "Say it again."

It didn't stick in his throat. Didn't hurt or feel wrong. "I love you."

He kissed her then. There, in the middle of chaos, on the floor and in unbelievable pain, he crossed his mouth over hers and kept going until she sagged in his arms.

Holden's face appeared right next to them. "Uh, hate to break this up."

Caleb opened one eye and then reluctantly put a bit of distance between his mouth and Avery's. "What?"

"We got some guys here who need first aid."

"Russell?" he asked.

Holden shook his head. "Didn't make it, but I'm guessing that was always Trevor's plan."

Caleb was about to shift positions and see if he could move his injured leg. Then he looked into Avery's bright face. Despite the exhaustion and fear, the injuries and the horrors around them, she had never looked more beautiful.

"You know what?" he whispered as he wrapped his arms around her waist.

Her eyes sparkled with mischief. "What?"

"I'm going to let them get this one." Then he lowered his head and kissed her again.

Chapter Nineteen

"I'm not doing this every night, you know." Avery made the comment later when the warehouse was dark and quiet and she massaged Caleb's leg. He had sprawled diagonally across the mattress and groaned with delight at her soft touch against the parts of his leg that didn't ache.

When she heard the appreciative sounds rumbling up his throat, she knew she'd do whatever he wanted. It helped that he spent the past twelve hours professing his love. He said it to her in front of everyone and even announced it to the nurses at the hospital as they checked out his reinjured knee.

"Have I told you how much I love your hands?" His voice was muffled because he had an arm thrown over his face.

"I bet you'd say that to anyone who massaged your leg right now."

He raised his arm and his head. "If Zach touched me I'd punch him."

"Nice."

"I love you."

She smiled, hugging the comment close to her heart. "I know."

"I don't even get to hear it back anymore." Caleb flopped on his back, sounding extremely pathetic. "One day and I'm taken for granted."

She knew he was kidding. Still, she loved to torment him. "I don't feel like it."

"Just wait until I can get up and chase you around."

"Until then we'll have to think of other ways to entertain ourselves."

"This one is good."

She let her hand slip up his thigh as she moved her body higher on the bed. When she glanced up, he was staring at her.

The amusement had left his face. "I do love you, you know."

"And I love you." Her fingers tangled in his belt. "Now lie back and let me show you."

A huge smile filled his face. "I love it when you take charge."

"Then you are about to have a fantastic hour." And a fantastic life. She would make sure of it.

TREVOR DIDN'T KNOW WHY John insisted they meet on the steps of the Capitol. Seemed a bit dramatic. He assumed the location indicated John's mistrust of Orion's offices. He probably worried Trevor would tape their conversation, which he would. It paid to collect information. With Bram gone and the Russell situation neutralized, Trevor could put the entire episode behind him.

He had learned something. He'd never be blackmailed again.

"You're early," John said.

"Call it a habit." That's exactly what it was. "I admit to being curious about your request."

John glanced around, then frowned. "I found it."

"What?"

"I have the tape."

Trevor felt his blood drain from his face. "I don't know what—"

"Let's not play games, Trevor. I've listened to it. Amazing what you can learn about a man's character when he's under fire. Almost makes me worry for your ex-wife's safety."

Trevor struggled with the best way to handle the situation. He hadn't been prepared for this news. For this shock. "As you know, she's very much alive."

"For now."

Trevor could feel his life slipping out of his control. "What are we doing here, John?"

"You didn't actually think Russell was the top of the food chain, did you?"

The shocks just kept coming. As soon as Trevor regained his balance and started breathing again, John hit him with something new. "Meaning?"

"I was his security. I held the tape the entire time. Figured it would be the perfect way to get you to do my bidding." John laughed. "What, you haven't figured it out? You thought Russell was controlling Bram? You can't be serious."

"No."

"Of course not. Russell was weak, hampered by an oversize ego."

Trevor didn't say anything. Didn't move. Inside rage built until his muscles ached with the need to pound John into the ground. On the outside, he refused to let it show. He knew from experience the longer he stayed quiet, the more he would learn.

John seemed determined to share his information, and Trevor let him. Later Trevor would assess.

Then he would plan.

AVERY LOOKED AT LUKE over the top of her coffee cup the next morning. "Why aren't we pulling Adam in from West Virginia?"

Caleb loved that she said we. She fit in with Recovery as though she'd always been there. She had a job to go back to but for right now, she wasn't in a rush. She said she was content to be with him, and he wasn't arguing.

"Maddie isn't safe yet," he explained.

She shot him a surprised look. "How do you figure that?"

"Let's say we're not sure we have all the players in this game," Luke said. "Trevor clearly is in deeper than we thought."

Zach took the seat across from Avery. "And we still don't know where Rod is."

Her frown deepened. "So, what do we do?"

Caleb knew the answer. It was one of the things they did best. "We wait."

"And Adam gets stuck fifty miles away." She seemed particularly disgruntled on Adam's behalf.

Zach laughed. "He's doing okay."

Avery froze while taking another sip of coffee. "Just how pretty is Maddie?"

"Very," Zach said.

Luke got up and kissed Avery on the forehead. "Now, if you'll excuse me, I'm going home to my wife."

Caleb got it now. The need to rush home to a woman, to be with her all the time. He put an arm around Avery's shoulders. "We'll protect the warehouse."

Luke waved as he walked with Zach to the door. "Just make sure it's standing this time tomorrow."

"I think we can manage," Avery whispered to Caleb.

He kissed her. "Yeah, we manage just fine."

* * * * *

Harlequin

INTRIGUE

COMING NEXT MONTH

Available March 8, 2011

#1263 RANSOM FOR A PRINCE
Cowboys Royale
Lisa Childs

#1264 AK-COWBOY
Sons of Troy Ledger
Joanna Wayne

#1265 THE SECRET OF CYPRIERE BAYOU
Shivers
Jana DeLeon

#1266 PROTECTING PLAIN JANE
The Precinct: SWAT
Julie Miller

#1267 NAVY SEAL SECURITY
Brothers in Arms
Carol Ericson

#1268 CIRCUMSTANTIAL MARRIAGE
Thriller
Kerry Connor

REQUEST YOUR FREE BOOKS!
2 FREE NOVELS PLUS 2 FREE GIFTS!

♦Harlequin®

INTRIGUE®

BREATHTAKING ROMANTIC SUSPENSE

YES! Please send me 2 FREE Harlequin Intrigue® novels and my 2 FREE gifts (gifts are worth about $10). After receiving them, if I don't wish to receive any more books, I can return the shipping statement marked "cancel." If I don't cancel, I will receive 6 brand-new novels every month and be billed just $4.24 per book in the U.S. or $4.99 per book in Canada. That's a saving of at least 15% off the cover price! It's quite a bargain! Shipping and handling is just 50¢ per book in the U.S. and 75¢ per book in Canada.* I understand that accepting the 2 free books and gifts places me under no obligation to buy anything. I can always return a shipment and cancel at any time. Even if I never buy another book, the two free books and gifts are mine to keep forever.

182/382 HDN FC5H

Name _____ (PLEASE PRINT)

Address _____ Apt. #

City _____ State/Prov. _____ Zip/Postal Code

Signature (if under 18, a parent or guardian must sign)

Mail to the **Reader Service:**
IN U.S.A.: P.O. Box 1867, Buffalo, NY 14240-1867
IN CANADA: P.O. Box 609, Fort Erie, Ontario L2A 5X3

Not valid for current subscribers to Harlequin Intrigue books.

**Are you a subscriber to Harlequin Intrigue books
and want to receive the larger-print edition?
Call 1-800-873-8635 or visit www.ReaderService.com.**

* Terms and prices subject to change without notice. Prices do not include applicable taxes. Sales tax applicable in N.Y. Canadian residents will be charged applicable taxes. Offer not valid in Quebec. This offer is limited to one order per household. All orders subject to credit approval. Credit or debit balances in a customer's account(s) may be offset by any other outstanding balance owed by or to the customer. Please allow 4 to 6 weeks for delivery. Offer available while quantities last.

Your Privacy—The Reader Service is committed to protecting your privacy. Our Privacy Policy is available online at www.ReaderService.com or upon request from the Reader Service.

We make a portion of our mailing list available to reputable third parties that offer products we believe may interest you. If you prefer that we not exchange your name with third parties, or if you wish to clarify or modify your communication preferences, please visit us at www.ReaderService.com/consumerschoice or write to us at Reader Service Preference Service, P.O. Box 9062, Buffalo, NY 14269. Include your complete name and address.

JEMIMA yanked open a drawer in the sideboard to find Alfie's birth certificate. Her son was her husband's child. It was a question of telling the truth whether she liked it or not. She extended the certificate to Alejandro.

"This has to be nonsense," Alejandro asserted.

"Well, if you can find some other way of explaining how I managed to give birth by that date and Alfie not be yours, I'd like to hear it," Jemima challenged.

Alejandro glanced up, golden eyes bright as blades and as dangerous. "All this proves is that you must still have been pregnant when you walked out on our marriage. It does not automatically follow that the child is mine."

"'I know it doesn't suit you to hear this news now and I really didn't want to tell you. But I can't lie to you about it. Someday Alfie may want to look you up and get acquainted."

"If what you have just told me is the truth, if that little boy does prove to be mine, it was vindictive and extremely selfish of you to leave me in ignorance!"

Jemima paled. "When I left you, I had no idea that I was still pregnant."

"Two years is a long period of time, yet you made no attempt to inform me that I might be a father. I will want DNA tests to confirm your claim before I make any decision about what I want to do."

"Do as you like," she told him curtly. "*I* know who Alfie's father is and there has never been any doubt of his identity."

"I will make arrangements for the tests to be carried out and I will see you again when the result is available," Alejandro drawled with lashings of dark Spanish masculine reserve.

"I'll contact a solicitor and start the divorce," Jemima proffered in turn.

Alejandro's eyes narrowed in a piercing scrutiny that made her uncomfortable. "It would be foolish to do anything before we have that DNA result."

"I disagree," Jemima flashed back. "I should have applied for a divorce the minute I left you!"

Alejandro quirked an ebony brow. "And why didn't you?"

Jemima dealt him a fulminating glance but said nothing, merely moving past him to open her front door in a blunt invitation for him to leave.

"I'll be in touch," he delivered on the doorstep.

What is Alejandro's next move? Perhaps rekindling their marriage is the only solution! But will Jemima agree?

Find out in Lynne Graham's
exciting new romance
JEMIMA'S SECRET

Available March 2011
from Harlequin Presents®.

Start your Best Body today with these top 3 nutrition tips!

1. SHOP THE PERIMETER OF THE GROCERY STORE: The good stuff—fruits, veggies, lean proteins and dairy—always line the outer edges of the store. When you veer into the center aisles, you enter the temptation zone, where the unhealthy foods live.

2. WATCH PORTION SIZES: Most portion sizes in restaurants are nearly twice the size of a true serving and at home, it's easy to "clean your plate." Use these easy serving guidelines:
- Protein: the palm of your hand
- Grains or Fruit: a cup of your hand
- Veggies: the palm of two open hands

3. USE THE RAINBOW RULE FOR PRODUCE: Your produce drawers should be filled with every color of fruits and vegetables. The greater the variety, the more vitamins and other nutrients you add to your diet.

Find these and many more helpful tips in

YOUR BEST BODY NOW
by
TOSCA RENO
WITH STACY BAKER

Bestselling Author of THE EAT-CLEAN DIET

Available wherever books are sold!

NTRSERIESFEB

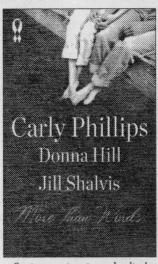